D1502442

NETWORK VENTURES, INC.
4901 Atkins Road
Cary, NC 27511

Reubella and
the Old Focus Home

Reubella and the Old Focus Home

Suzanne Newton

W

The Westminster Press

Philadelphia

COPYRIGHT©1978 SUZANNE NEWTON

First edition

PUBLISHED BY THE WESTMINSTER PRESS®
PHILADELPHIA, PENNSYLVANIA

Printed in the United States of America
9 8 7 6 5 4 3 2 1

Library of Congress Cataloging in Publication Data

Newton, Suzanne.
Reubella and the Old Focus Home.

SUMMARY: Three vivacious elderly ladies turn life in a
sleepy southern town upside down.
[1. Old age—Fiction] I. Title.
PZ7.N4875Re   [Fic]   78–18336
ISBN 0–664–32635–8

For Mary Ann, Sherry, and Mel
Best Friends
and for Heather, who let me
borrow
her idea

I stood at the top of the arch of Peaceful River bridge and took a last look downriver toward our house. There it sat, brighter and bigger than any of the others lining the shore—the color of margarine. It was an architectural spectacle, thanks to Dad, who had said, when we first came to Shad four years ago, that if the Foster Lodge and Tourist Home was going to be profitable, we would have to call attention to it in some way.

The problem was that most of the people coming across the bridge lived in Shad already and were not looking for overnight lodging. Shad was a coastal town not located on the beaten path of tourism. Dad's grand scheme was perishing for lack of customers.

I did not want to leave. I liked school and had been elected to the Student Council. Because I am five feet eight and a half inches tall I also had a good chance of making the girls basketball team which our school was going to have this year for the first time in thirty years. I liked the town and the people, who had been neighborly and tolerant, not to mention downright friendly. I was going to miss Debbie Claymore, my very best friend in the world, who did not even know I was going away. And to make matters more difficult, it was a clear blue-

and-orange day that makes even a town like Shad look good. The river sparkled, inviting me to stay around.

For a dangerous instant I almost chickened out, but after a couple of deep breaths the feeling passed. There was no help for it. Nothing was going to change. I turned away from Shad and started down the incline to the other side.

To tell the truth, things were kind of blurry and I was looking down at my feet when I heard the car engine. I stopped walking, stepped up on the curbing, and leaned against the concrete rail again, pretending to be looking out over the river. Maybe whoever it was would go by fast enough not to notice me.

The engine chugged on up the incline. To my dismay it began to slow down as it approached and then came to a halt, idling right at my back.

Oh, brother! I thought as I turned around, all set to smile and tell whatever fibs were necessary. But what I saw wiped my mind perfectly blank.

It was a converted postal van—I could tell by the shape and by the fact that the steering mechanism was on the right instead of the left. Only it wasn't red, white, and blue anymore, but a metallic aquamarine with weird pictures painted on the side.

What really got me, though, was the person driving.

"Good afternoon," she said in a voice that could command a regiment. She wore a white silk blouse, jodphurs, and leather boots—I could see all this because she had slid the door open in order to speak to me. Bone earrings dangled almost to her shoulders, and on her head she wore a pith helmet. A chiffon scarf with the two ends drifting loose was looped around its crown. Her silver hair and wrinkles indicated she was old, but her eyes were dark and unclouded.

"Do you live around here?" she asked me.

I nodded, gripping the concrete rail.

"Good! We're looking for lodging for the night. Perhaps you could tell us where we might go?"

I didn't see anyone else with her, but any number of people could be hiding in the van. I was seized by conflicting emotions. Could Dad handle a bunch of guests without me? It was a sobering thought—he had never done it before.

I cleared my throat, to make sure my voice didn't come out too wispy. "If you'll look over yonder, you'll see a big yellow house. It's a tourist home. You can stay there for a reasonable fee."

The woman shaded her eyes and followed my pointing finger.

"Heavens!" she exclaimed. "What an amazing building!"

At that moment I heard stirring noises in the rear of the van, and a little elderly lady with tinted goggle glasses peeped around the side door, giving me a smile so wide that her eyes almost closed. Orange hair flamed around her face in violent curls.

"Hel-lo!" she said in two musical notes like a birdcall. "Are you ready?"

I didn't know whether I was ready or not.

The orange-haired lady stepped into full view. She was wearing a purple velvet jump suit appliquéd with large satin flowers the same color as her hair.

I am sure I stared. She twirled about, still grinning. "Do you like it?"

"Well," I said, "it's all right. But I would advise you to be careful where you wear it. It could cause a riot in a place like Shad."

From inside the van someone as yet invisible began to laugh, peal after peal. The safari lady joined in with a sort of bray, while Orange Hair giggled and covered her mouth with her hand.

Nobody likes being made fun of. I began to inch my

way along the rail. They were as nutty as fruitcakes. The invisible person was likely the craziest of all.

"Oh!" said Orange Hair. "Are you leaving?"

I motioned in the direction of Ferris. "Yes, ma'am. And I'm late. Good-by." Then just as I was about even with the rear bumper of the van, the back door slid open and I found myself jaw to jaw with the third individual.

This one looked more like a regular person. She was of medium height and slight build, and her gray hair was pulled back in an ordinary-looking bun. She could have been anyone's grandmother. Her spectacles hung about her neck on a beaded chain. The most unusual thing about her was that she was dressed in black—black shoes, hose, skirt, and blouse, with a large red bow at the collar.

"How d'you do?" she said, sticking out her hand. "My name is Nesselrode—Hollis Nesselrode."

I shook the hand and said hello because I didn't know what else to do. It was a small bony hand, like velvet-covered twigs.

"Holly, do see if you can talk the young lady into going into town with us!" the safari woman called.

"I can't do that," I said, before the Nesselrode person could say anything. "I'm going that way—to Ferris."

"An errand?" asked Ms. Nesselrode.

Lying has never come easy for me, especially when I haven't planned ahead of time to do it. I shook my head.

"Oh. Running away, then?"

I shifted from one foot to the other.

"I've run away a few times in my day," Ms. Nesselrode said. "Sometimes it is necessary."

I looked at her. I have read a few psychology books myself. However, as best I could tell, she was just stating a fact.

"Well, I have to be going," I said, and then, because I felt somewhat guilty, I added, "The man who runs the Foster Lodge and Tourist Home is my dad. Offer him ten dollars for the night for the three of you. He will try to up the price, but just be firm. He'll come around."

"Thank you," said Ms. Nesselrode.

"And I'd appreciate it if you wouldn't let on that you saw me. I need a head start. He won't miss me much until it's time to do the supper dishes."

The safari lady cut off the engine, pulled up the emergency brake, and came back to where Ms. Nesselrode and I were. The orange-haired lady leaned out the side door to listen, the legs of her jump suit whipping in the river breeze. I stepped back. I had no doubt that with my long legs I could outrun a bunch of grandmothers, but still—

"I'm Constance Cromwell," said the safari lady.

"Ernestine Smithers," said Orange Hair with a little wave of her hand.

I bobbed my head.

Ms. Nesselrode chewed on her underlip. "I wonder, Miss Foster, if we might do each other a favor?"

It startled me that she had picked up my last name. "I . . . I don't think so, since I'm leaving."

"We do need to stop here tonight," she went on as though I hadn't said a word. "Frankly, I would feel much more comfortable dealing with your father if you were there too. Could you possibly reconsider? Then tomorrow, when we start on our way again, we will take you wherever you want to go in Buxtehude."

"Buxtehude is the van," Ms. Smithers explained.

I looked at the river and thought how much I was going to miss it. I thought about the nine-mile hike to Ferris and spending the night in the bus station there. I also thought about the three ladies at the mercy of Dad's incompetence. He would forget to put out clean towels, and he was not a good cook—that's all there was to it.

"How do I know I can trust you not to tell on me?"

"It would be dishonorable for us to betray you." Ms. Cromwell drew herself up.

My insides struggled for a few seconds more and then gave in. Getting a ride in the Buxty Hooda thing would be better than riding the bus. Also cheaper. I'd get to Raleigh just as soon and get a good night's sleep in my own bed besides.

"All right," I said. "If you'll take me to Raleigh tomorrow."

"Agreed." Ms. Nesselrode put out her hand again. "Let me help you—the step's a bit high."

I took hold of the bony little hand and was pulled up into the van as though I were no heavier than a piece of cotton.

"Gosh, you're strong! I weigh a hundred and thirty-five pounds with this knapsack."

Ms. Cromwell brayed again. "Holly was a concert pianist and orchestra conductor until she retired. Her muscles are made of steel bands and piano wire."

"Now, Constance—stop exaggerating!" Ms. Nesselrode seemed embarrassed. She bent her head back so as to look me in the eye. "You are quite tall," she observed.

"Yes, ma'am. I know. Being little and cute would be about as hard for me as for a giraffe to hide behind a telephone pole."

"It would be difficult," Ms. Cromwell murmured.

"I have accepted the fact that parts of me will always stick out," I said, slipping the heavy knapsack off my shoulders, "so I may as well stay in the open to begin with."

"Well, I hope Buxtehude won't cramp your style too much." Ms. Cromwell went back to the driver's seat. Ms. Smithers pulled her head inside. Ms. Nesselrode slid the rear door shut again, and I stared.

The Buxty Hooda was carpeted with orange shag rug. A pinned-back curtain of orange and brown print hung midway, to separate the leather seats in front from the rest of the van. I saw a jumble of luggage and boxes, a table, a built-in sink, two oil paintings facing each other from opposite sides, and—this is hard to believe—a crystal chandelier hanging from the central light fixture. Its dangling pieces brushed the top of Ms. Smithers' head, producing a tinkling noise that made me think of invisible people laughing.

"The chandelier was Ernestine's idea," Ms. Nesselrode explained. "She found it in Madrid. It's a bit bulky for these quarters, but it sounds nice, don't you think?"

I was sure it didn't matter what I thought. I made my way forward around the boxes and luggage and sat in the seat beside Ms. Cromwell. Ms. Nesselrode and Ms. Smithers sat behind us. Ms. Cromwell started the motor and the van moved slowly over the arch of the bridge and down the incline toward Shad.

"Since we've settled on this arrangement, I think we should be on a first-name basis," Ms. Cromwell said. The chiffon veil fluttered in the breeze from the open window. "You can call me Connie—and that's Holly. And Ernestine prefers to be called by her whole name. 'Ernie' and 'Teeny' are too misleading."

"I don't think I can do that," I said. "It doesn't seem respectful."

"Well, do you wish to be called 'Miss Foster'?"

I felt myself turning red. "No, ma'am. My name's Reubella. R-e-u-b-e-l-l-a. I was named for my grandparents, Reuben and Ella Foster. My mom and dad didn't know, when they named me, that there was a virus by a similar name."

I expected them to burst out laughing again, but they didn't. Instead they murmured polite things like "What an interesting name!" "Unusual!" and so forth.

"It isn't easy going through life with a name like a virus," I told them, "but I have tried not to let it be an obstacle between me and my goals. I don't answer to a nickname. If people are interested in communicating with me, they have to use my real name."

"That's very admirable," said Ms. Nesselrode. "What are your goals?"

I did not reply right away. After all, I didn't know these women and I wasn't sure my goals were any of their business.

"Well, I don't know that I want to talk about all of them. But one of them, for sure, is not to live a hand-to-mouth existence anymore. It can wear a person out."

Ms. Cromwell nodded understandingly. "Do you think that your . . . ah . . . excursion to Raleigh will provide you some security?"

"I'm not sure," I said, "but things couldn't be any more insecure than they are right now. At least if I get a job and earn some money, I'll be the only one spending it."

We had gotten into town by that time and were cruising along the main street, which runs parallel to the river. A number of people were out on the sidewalks standing around, because Saturday is the day when farmers come in for supplies. They usually stay to see the movie, which has one showing at seven P.M. Out of the corner of my eye I could tell that the Buxty Hooda was causing quite a sensation. People would see it, and then they would keep on staring as we passed, saying things to each other and pointing.

The three ladies made no effort to be inconspicuous. To my amazement, Ms. Cromwell stood up to drive—which is something you can do in a postal van—waving at the populace with one hand while she steered with the other. Ms. Smithers wafted her handkerchief and smiled. Ms. Nesselrode bowed from side to side as though she were the queen of England. I stared straight ahead and hoped no one would recognize me.

"Is it just you and your father?" Ms. Smithers asked, tapping me on the shoulder.

I nodded. "It's been he and I since I was five. I don't know where my mom is, but he tells me she got married to somebody else." I didn't look at any of them. I didn't want to see those sad-eyed expressions ladies give me when they find out I don't have a mother. Dad says he used to get those kinds of looks, too, when he was a boy. He has always advised me to be tough about it.

"I can certainly understand *why* she married somebody else," I went on. "My dad is a nice person, but living with him on a day-to-day basis is something else. He is a reasonably good dad, but he isn't much of a manager."

"Oh," said Ms. Nesselrode. "Does he drink and carouse?"

"Oh, no! It's just that he isn't farsighted. He doesn't plan anything. Every day for him is separate from every other day—"

I stopped, realizing that I was getting louder and more passionate, and was astonished at myself, never having expressed these feelings to anyone except Debbie Claymore. It seemed a good time to change the subject.

"I just thought of something," I said. "Suppose you weren't planning to go in the direction of Raleigh. Maybe you were going to the beach or some other place?"

"Actually, we can go where we please," Ms. Nesselrode said. "We've no timetable and no itinerary. Taking you to Raleigh will be as much of an adventure to us as what we had originally planned."

"Yes. You see, we're on a search," Ms. Smithers said, "and whereas we know what we're looking for, we have no idea where we shall find it. Every day and every place is a possibility."

"We shall know when we find it," Ms. Cromwell put in.

For a moment I had forgotten they were crazy, but this mysterious talk brought me back to reality. They sounded a lot like Dad.

Well, they seemed harmless enough. In return for seeing that they spent a comfortable night at Foster Lodge, I would get a comfortable ride to Raleigh. It was a fair trade. "I hope you will," I said politely. I pointed to the street that led to our house. "Turn off here."

The oystershells in our driveway made a loud, crunching noise as the van pulled up and parked in front of the Lodge. Dad heard the noise and came out immediately—the engine was still running when he appeared at the door, rubbing his hands together and smiling.

My dad is a personable man. A number of single ladies in Shad had been interested in him—a few might even have settled for him the way he was and been willing to make a living for both of them, but he continued to avoid marriage, which was probably best for all concerned. His charming nature caused people to expect more of him than he was willing to deliver. People were always getting disappointed on his account.

So I was wondering whether these three ladies would be watchful, or whether they would be taken in by his smoothness. If they were, I might not get my ride to Raleigh after all. They would be on his side instead of mine and would try to talk me into staying. I'd end up having to ride the bus anyway, and be a day later besides. All this flashed through my mind as I saw him come out smiling, rubbing his hands, and I got very uneasy. I had to resist the impulse to tell Ms. Cromwell to gun the motor and let's get out of there fast.

In the silence after she had turned off the engine, I climbed down from the van, holding the knapsack as inconspicuously as possible. If Dad didn't ask questions, I wouldn't have to tell any lies.

"I met these ladies coming into town," I told him. "They were looking for a place to stay the night."

"Well, you've certainly come to the right place!" He moved toward the van, holding out his hand. "Welcome to the Foster Lodge and Tourist Home!"

Ms. Cromwell gave him a bemused look, gazing down upon him as though she smelled something not quite fresh.

"I've never stayed in a Foster Home before," she said.

Just for an instant Dad faltered, then took himself in hand and laughed uproariously. "Wonderful! Marvelous sense of humor! I can tell we're going to enjoy having you here."

Ms. Smithers and Ms. Nesselrode looked thoughtful. None of the three made a move to get out of the van. I felt pulled in two directions at once.

"This is Ms. Constance Cromwell," I said, coming around to stand on the driver's side. "And that is Ms. Smithers and Ms. Nesselrode. This is my father, Stephen Foster."

"Heavens!" exclaimed Ms. Nesselrode. "Stephen Foster—like the songwriter?"

Dad ducked his head and gave his little smile. "Well —we have a first and last name in common. That's about all."

"Too bad," she sighed. "I thought perhaps you might be a fellow musician."

"He has a nice singing voice," I said.

"In my experience, talent is only a small part of what it takes," Ms. Nesselrode observed. "One needs discipline and a sense of purpose to be a true musician."

"I'm sure you're right about that." Dad's exuberance

had cooled some, although he was still smiling. "Could I carry your things inside?"

"Yes," I said hastily. "I'll show them to their rooms."

"All right. Just let me climb up there and I'll—"

"We'll hand out what you should carry," Ms. Cromwell said with unmistakable firmness.

"Of course. I didn't want you to . . . ah . . . strain your backs carrying something too heavy."

"We travel quite a bit—we've learned to put our few belongings in small bags and boxes."

Dad stood where he was, more subdued than I have seen him in a long time. He didn't seem to know what to do with his hands while he waited for the ladies to decide what to bring inside. While he was casting about, his eyes happened to fall on my knapsack, which was lying on the ground at my feet. His eyebrows climbed slightly.

"I say—were you running away?"

My heart squeezed up because I was going to have to tell a lie, or at least a piece of one. What I said surprised even me.

"Yes, I was—but I had second thoughts."

"Well, I'm certainly glad. I'll need your help tonight, since we have guests."

That was all he said. Part of me was glad he didn't take what I said seriously, because tomorrow I could leave for good and he could never say I hadn't told him. But another part of me was sad. I wished that he would miss me—myself, the person—and not just my usefulness.

"Here, Mr. Foster!" Ms. Smithers called. "Would you mind taking my reticule?"

She was hanging out of the van as she had done earlier, holding on with one hand, waving the thing she called a reticule in the other. Dad got a full view of her costume, and it almost rattled him.

"Yes, of course," he said in a stunned voice. She

handed down the bulging net shopping bag, which, from the way he took it, must have weighed a lot more than it appeared to.

"And you can carry this, too." Ms. Cromwell dragged a large canvas duffel bag and flung it out the rear door.

"I haven't anything but my shoulder purse," said Ms. Nesselrode. "I can manage."

While Dad struggled with the bags, I led the ladies inside. We had made a combination office and lobby of the wide front hall and living room. There was a fireplace and a lot of big overstuffed chairs. The three women looked about with frank curiosity, nodding their heads approvingly.

"Lovely!" exclaimed Ms. Nesselrode. They touched the walls and the old carved mantelpiece with sensitive fingers.

"It's quite perfect." Ms. Smithers' voice was hushed, as though she were in church. "Who would have thought it?"

"Miraculous!" said Ms. Cromwell.

Once again I came to my senses. These ladies, although not taken in by Dad's charm, were nevertheless strange—probably unstable. I went behind the desk and got out the guest register.

"Sign your names right here," I said, handing them book and pen. "We can provide rooms for all three of you for ten dollars. We can serve dinner and breakfast for a small extra charge. Payment in advance required." I was rattling off the speech Dad had made me learn four years before when we first opened the Lodge. The last sentence was out of my mouth before I realized how it must sound.

"Forget that last," I said, blushing. "You don't have to pay in advance."

"If it's the policy, then that's what we shall do." Ms. Nesselrode fished in her large black leather bag and brought out a bulging old-fashioned change purse. "How much with the two meals?"

I figured the cost and told her, and she handed me the money off a large roll of bills. It was at that moment Dad finally came through the doorway, wrestling with the reticule and duffel bag, no doubt cursing under his breath that these old ladies didn't use plain suitcases with handles like other people. He saw the transfer of money, and the roll of bills from which Ms. Nesselrode had counted it. I could see the glazed expression that always comes into his eyes when he thinks about Money and How To Get It. My heart sank.

I took out my wallet and put the money in it, Dad's eyes upon me the whole time. His professional image as an innkeeper kept him from saying anything in front of the ladies.

"Now," I said, "if you'll come upstairs, I'll show you your rooms."

They followed me up the wide, winding stairway. We had not been able to afford new carpet or stair treads, but I was not too sorry about that. The old maroon ones were good quality stuff, and even though they were thread-bare they fitted the house. Admittedly the musty odor of age hung over everything, but I had gotten used to it.

Most tourists who came to Foster Lodge turned up their noses and seldom came back a second time. It pleased me that these ladies were not turning up their noses or pulling themselves in so as not to touch things any more than necessary. They made little clucks and exclamations. Ms. Smithers said that we had some lovely antiques, which is something I did not know.

Five of the rooms on the second floor were on the side overlooking the river. One of them was mine, but the other four were reserved for guests, since Dad preferred to sleep in the little room next to the office downstairs. I gave each of the ladies one of the rooms overlooking the river, noting out of the corner of my eye that Dad, after he had brought up the reticule and duffel bag, lingered for a minute, but then went back downstairs.

I announced that dinner would be served at six thirty and left them in Ms. Cromwell's room, crowded around the large window and making ecstatic comments about the scenery. I made a point of going down as quietly as possible, with an eye to reaching the front door before Dad noticed, but he was sitting at the desk with his arms folded, waiting.

"Where do you think you're going, young lady?"

"To the store."

He came from behind the desk and held out his hand, palm up. "I saw you put the money in your wallet. You're supposed to put it in the cash drawer."

"So you can put it in *your* wallet?" I retorted. "Nope —there's no decent food in the house, and these ladies have paid in advance for two meals. I'm going to go buy groceries with part of the money."

"The money, Reubella."

I stood there, getting madder and madder. Maybe the fact that I'd be gone the next day gave me more courage than usual.

"No, sir. You can have what's left, after I buy food for dinner and breakfast."

"Reubella, you're not too old for a spanking!" He grabbed my shoulder and shook me, something he had not done in a long time. I was about to surrender the wallet, mostly because my feelings were hurt, when Ms. Cromwell's voice boomed from the stairs behind me.

"Mr. Foster!"

Dad seemed to wilt. He dropped his hand, attempting a smile for Ms. Cromwell's benefit. Her expression was like carved granite. Under the silver hair her dark eyes bored holes in his playacting until he just gave up. The fake smile disappeared and he stood there, looking ashamed.

"Mr. Foster, would you be so kind as to show me how the gas heaters in the rooms work?"

"Certainly. Be happy to." Without looking at me he followed her upstairs. I waited a moment and then went to the store as planned.

On the way there and back I kept thinking. Ms. Cromwell had not only seen through Dad's acting but had made him stop. It was amazing. In my experience no one had ever been able to bring it off. Dad was so in the habit of acting whenever there was an outside person around to be the audience that he had a hard time knowing when he was pretending and when he was being his rea' self. I wondered what effect it would have on his behavi.. the rest of the time the ladies were at the Lodge.

I am not a fancy cook, but I know how to fry chicken and things like that. I fixed a plain old country meal, which included—besides the chicken—green beans, mashed potatoes, biscuits, and baked apples. No doubt Dad would give me grief about it, since he would have served hot dogs and pork-and-beans to realize more of a profit. But I had already decided what to say to him. I would remind him that these three ladies were obviously well-to-do, that they were footloose and free, and that if he invested some capital in showing them real hospitality this time, they would surely come back and bring their friends. I thought it was a good argument, even though it wasn't likely to happen.

Dad did not want to eat with the guests, but then Ms. Cromwell came down and saw the table set for three.

"I wish to get better acquainted with you and your father," she said. Since her wishes were more like commands, I set two more places so the five of us could dine together.

Ms. Cromwell had changed into a black velvet pants suit that made her look something like Zorro without hat and mask. Ms. Smithers wore a billowing caftan whose color matched her hair, and Ms. Nesselrode had changed from all black to all white. Just to look at them would have been enough, without even carrying on any conversation, but there was a lot of that, too. Dinner that night was more like a banquet for twenty celebrities than a modest supper for three old ladies, a man, and a girl.

Dad can be clever when it suits his purposes. He took the offensive at the beginning and asked them what their destination was.

"Well, actually we don't have a destination Proper," Ms. Cromwell said.

"Or even *im*proper," Ms. Smithers put in with one of her eye-closing smiles. "We're on an Expedition."

"It must be very nice to be retired and wealthy so you can travel about and see the world at your leisure," said Dad.

Ms. Cromwell shrugged. "Oh, I don't know—we've seen most of the world two or three times over. Some of it was worth seeing, some not."

"One thing we have learned," said Ms. Smithers, "is that *where* one is makes less difference than what sort of person one is. Adventure is everywhere, but not everyone is aware of it."

"Yes." Ms. Cromwell nodded vigorously. "When my camel died under me in the Moroccan desert, I remember thinking, 'I'm having an adventure.' My greatest concern was that I might not return to tell anyone that I had had it. *Where* it happened was of less consequence than the fact that *I* was having it and that it taught me something about myself that I hadn't known before."

"Which was . . . ?"

"That I have strong survival instincts."

"Of course, you have to be willing to risk in order to

make yourself open to adventure," Ms. Nesselrode said. "Just before World War II, I smuggled some important documents out of Norway to the United States in my Steinway grand. I had to play the part of an irascible person—complained to the ship's captain constantly about the terrible care his crew was taking of my piano. I insisted on going down to check it each day in the storage area. The poor captain was so thankful to see me get off the boat in New York! That adventure was difficult for me. I don't relish being unlikable."

"Didn't the captain ever find out you weren't really like that?" I asked.

She chuckled. "Years later, after the war, I ran into him in the Bahamas. I had the opportunity to tell him why I had acted so rudely. He was very forgiving."

"The thing about adventure is its unexpected nature," said Ms. Smithers. "Therefore you have to be prepared to enter into it with whatever tools or properties you have on hand."

"You mean such as using bobby pins to pick locks?" Dad prompted.

"Well . . . yes, only not always so obvious as that. I carry most of my worldly goods in my reticule—just the few things I truly care about. My paints and canvases and bath oil and a couple of changes of clothes."

"And some rocks," Dad muttered under his breath, but I think I was the only one who heard him.

"Ernestine is a very fine painter," Ms. Cromwell told us. "She's much in demand as a portraitist."

"I was at the Louvre once studying a particular portrait I wanted to copy, when I saw two men hurrying down the corridor in my direction. I thought they looked rather furtive, to tell the truth. So without even thinking, I took the bath oil out of my reticule and poured it on the floor. Naturally, they slipped and fell—and one of them dropped a rolled canvas concealed under his coat."

"And the Louvre still has its painting of 'The Lace-maker,' thanks to Ernestine." Ms. Cromwell patted her friend's hand proudly.

My head spun, listening to their tales. It had to be lies. I could not believe that people who had really lived such adventurous lives would end up riding a remodeled postal van up and down the bleaknesses of eastern North Carolina. I looked at Dad and saw my own skepticism reflected in his eyes.

"So now you rove about, seeking adventure—is that right?" he asked.

Ms. Cromwell frowned. "Not exactly. No—that isn't what we're seeking."

There was an extended silence. The three ladies devoted their entire attention to their food, making exclamations about how good it was and all. Then Ms. Nesselrode cleverly turned the questions around and got Dad to talk about himself, which was his favorite subject. It was all right with me. I had more practical matters to deal with, such as getting to Raleigh and finding a job.

Sunday promised to be another fine day, the kind that would be cool in the shade, dry-hot in the sun. The morning breeze coming in my window smelled nicely of oysters and other fishy things. I felt a touch of sadness as I dressed and brushed my hair, wondering whether I could survive in the city without the river to look at and to smell. It would be a long time before I could come back to Shad. In the city I might become like a jellyfish laid up on a pier to dry in the sun, getting smaller and smaller until there would be nothing left but my outline, smelling faintly of river things. It was a chilling thought. I banged the brush down on the bureau and hurried to the kitchen.

Since I didn't really trust Dad to prepare the kind of breakfast I thought the three ladies deserved, I had told him he could sleep late and I'd be responsible. As I expected, he offered no objection. I fixed everything I could think of—eggs, bacon, toast, jelly, orange juice, and coffee. To my surprise, just as I was about to call the ladies, Dad wandered into the kitchen, sleepy-eyed but fully dressed.

"What made you get up so early?" I asked.

"Because I haven't smelled a breakfast like this in

months. My stomach was growling so loudly it woke me up and I couldn't go back to sleep."

I laughed and set another place at the table. Maybe if I cooked like this every morning, he would get up early and get started at doing something purposeful. Then I remembered it was my last morning. From now on he could sleep all day *and* all night if he pleased.

For all that the previous day had taught me, I was not prepared for the spectacle the ladies presented as they came one by one into the dining room. Ernestine Smithers wore red satin, which clashed with her hair color. Around her neck hung strands of beads, chains, heavy medallions, and chokers. She looked like the lone model in a jewelry store who had to display all the merchandise. On her fingers were rings of gold and silver, set with turquoise, opal, and ruby. She beamed at Dad and me, then sat at her place, blazing quietly like a constant candle.

Ms. Cromwell, in tweed pants and jacket, sported an orange cravat and a pair of copper earrings. Hollis Nesselrode was in gray wool with white collar and cuffs and a full skirt that was too long. For a moment after they had settled in their places there was silence. The kitchen fairly throbbed, like the vibrations of a boat's engines below deck. Then Ms. Smithers said:

"I should like to offer grace, if you wouldn't be offended."

Such things as grace at table give Dad great discomfort. Once at a P.T.A. meeting he was asked to pray, and nearly had a stroke. He confessed to me later that all he could think of was "Now I lay me down to sleep." However, I couldn't see that it would do any harm, particularly since he didn't have to say anything.

"We'd be pleased," I said.

"Then could we join hands?"

I held Constance Cromwell's iron paw in my right

hand and Dad's sweaty one in my left. It gave me an unbalanced feeling.

Ms. Smithers' grace was direct and simple. It had no Thees and Thous in it. She was not coy with God. She thanked Him that they had found the Foster Lodge and Tourist Home as some ancient pilgrim might have offered thanks for safe arrival in Jerusalem. She thanked Him for us Fosters and for the food. Last of all she implored His blessing upon their Search, which she did not name to Him but which, apparently, He already knew something about. Then she said Amen.

Dad had a thoughtful look on his face when we all raised our heads.

"We would like to attend church services somewhere this morning," Ms. Cromwell announced.

I lowered the fork I had just raised to my mouth and almost blurted, But I thought we were leaving for Raleigh! That would have been a stupid thing to do, however, right there in front of Dad.

He harrumphed and squirmed, since he does not keep up with churchly things. Still, he didn't want to look like a heathen in the eyes of these rich ladies.

"Reubella," he said, "why don't you tell them about the—ah—possibilities while I go out front to pick up the newspaper?"

I was glad he left the room, albeit with a cowardly excuse. As soon as he was out of earshot I said, "When are we leaving?"

The three women exchanged looks. "What about after lunch—will that be agreeable?" Ms. Nesselrode asked.

"I guess it'll have to be." I did not try to hide my irritation. They knew I was anxious to get out of town.

"We always attend services," Ms. Smithers said timidly. "Could you tell us where we might go?"

"There's the Methodist up the street a little way, but their preacher won't be here today—he only comes two

Sundays a month. The Episcopal is on the next street over. You can get to it quicker by going through Mrs. Bendix' cornfield if you don't mind getting dirt in your shoes. The Baptists are up near the fire station."

My last remark set them hooting with laughter, although I saw nothing funny about it. I was, in fact, feeling somewhat put out with them and had begun to entertain notions of taking up my knapsack and departing on foot as soon as I washed the breakfast dishes.

"Would you accompany us to the Episcopal Church?" Ms. Cromwell said.

"No," I said. "I have other things to do."

Thus when, an hour or so later, I found myself trudging through Mrs. Bendix' cornfield single file behind the three, I wondered if I had taken leave of my senses or if perhaps they were practicing witches who were so powerful I didn't have a chance against them.

My only good reason for coming along was that my friend Debbie Claymore is an Episcopalian and I would get to see her one more time before going away. And I must confess, too, that the idea of riding all the way to Raleigh appealed to me more than hiking to Ferris and catching a bus.

Ms. Smithers had added to her costume some elbow-length black gloves and a floppy, wide-brimmed hat. Ms. Cromwell, who disdained hats, had fastened her silver hair with a fancy comb from the Middle East. Ms. Nesselrode, in her gray outfit, resembled a faded nun. I felt as though I were going to a masquerade party instead of to church.

"It's rather different, walking through a cornfield to church," Ms. Smithers trilled, tottering a little on her patent leather heels.

"I told you," I said grumpily, but no one heard me. I stumbled along, bringing up the rear, keeping my eyes on the ground so as to prevent my good shoes from getting any dirtier than necessary. Their conversation seemed to skip over great gaps of detail, like mountain goats I'd seen on Walt Disney leaping from crag to crag. They had lived around each other so much they could speak shorthand. Half the time I didn't know what they were talking about.

The lumpy black dirt found its way into my shoes in spite of all I could do. Bugs flew up from the dried cornstalks and buzzed around my head. Only the thought that by nightfall I would be far away gave me any cheer.

"Tell me, Reubella—have you had second thoughts?"

Ms. Nesselrode's question was completely unexpected. She had stopped in her tracks and I almost ran into her. I shook my head.

"No, ma'am."

"Shad is a lovely town. It must be hard for you to go away."

I set my jaw. "A person can't always do what she wants to. Sometimes what's best for you isn't what you really want to do."

"True. But it seems a shame."

She stopped talking and resumed her progress along the row of corn. I was glad, because in my wishy-washy state of mind I didn't need anyone trying to talk me out of my plan.

When Ms. Nesselrode and I came out at the far side of the field, Ms. Smithers and Ms. Cromwell were already standing in the cool gray shade of the Episcopal cemetery. Ms. Smithers wiped the dust from her shoes with a lace handkerchief, which she then offered to the rest of us.

Beyond the cemetery was the churchyard, and there the congregation had gathered as it usually did before services, for chatting and catching up on the local news. I saw Debbie with her mother and father and decided the easiest thing would be to introduce the three ladies to them and let the grown-ups take over from there.

However, I had not counted on the effect Ms. Smithers, Ms. Cromwell, and Ms. Nesselrode would have as they advanced, smiling, upon the people. The crowd parted and literally moved back, as before an army. It dawned on me that we would have to stop where we were and negotiate, otherwise the people would retreat right on out of the churchyard.

As it turned out, Fate intervened in the person of the sexton, who chose that moment to ring the bell for worship to begin. Everyone turned and trooped inside with a great air of relief and a few nervous looks in our direction. Even Debbie, although she flashed me a big smile, didn't seem to know exactly what to do. All of this made me look at the three ladies again—really hard. Were they that strange, after all? I remembered how I'd felt on the bridge the day before. I'd have to bear in mind that I had had nearly twenty-four hours' exposure to get used to them.

Because Ms. Smithers was in the lead, we ended up sitting in the next-to-first pew, where we couldn't see anything but the altar and the minister, but we could *be* seen by everyone in the church. My back felt all the pairs of eyes staring and staring.

The acolytes and the Reverend Mr. Hawkes came up the aisle during the processional hymn. I wondered with some dread how he was going to react when, upon turning from facing the altar, he got his first look at the congregation and especially the next-to-first pew. I like Mr. Hawkes. He is a thin-nosed middle-aged person with anxious eyes. I didn't like to feel responsible for making him any more anxious than he already was.

St. James's congregation is not a large one, so anyone halfway singing can be heard. Ms. Cromwell, it turned out, sang everything an octave lower than women usually do. Her voice blared out loud and clear on "Holy, Holy,

Holy," although not always note-perfect. Ms. Nesselrode and Ms. Smithers had quavery soprano voices. I couldn't tell, standing beside them, whether I was singing or not. My face burned, though, and at one point during the hymn Ms. Nesselrode leaned over and asked whether I felt feverish.

At the end of the hymn we sat down and the readings and prayers began. I am not by nature or upbringing an Episcopalian, but have attended the services enough since coming to Shad to be able to follow the prayerbook fairly well. I expected to have to point out the place to the ladies, but right away I noticed Ms. Nesselrode didn't even need the book. She knew the prayer and the reading from the Psalms and the New Testament reading. Since it was just an ordinary Sunday, I could only suppose that she knew the whole prayerbook by heart. While I was pondering that enormous feat, we were called upon to pray. I always just bow my head, but Ms. Smithers knelt upon the bench. The beads and chains around her neck banged and jangled against the pew in front. I squinched my eyes tight and prayed fervently that she would not move during the prayer.

As I had feared, Mr. Hawkes was startled by what he found facing him in the person of the three strange ladies. He coped by keeping his eyes glued to the prayerbook and not looking up very much. I wished that we had either stayed home or gone to the Baptist church, where the ladies would have been less conspicuous. During the sermon I found it hard to concentrate on what Mr. Hawkes was saying because of what he was going through. Ms. Nesselrode nodded her head if she agreed with the point he was making, or shook it if she didn't. He was not used to such an outright response to his thinking. He kept losing his place and stumbling over words.

When the service was finally over and we emerged

into the noonday sunshine, I was perspiring heavily. So was Ms. Cromwell, but for different reasons.

"I'm not used to the Episcopal service," she confided. "All this kneeling and standing and sitting—not to mention thumbing through the prayerbook to find the place. For me it's just plain work! I make a much better Baptist."

Ms. Nesselrode lost no time in going up to Mr. Hawkes and taking his hand in the same grip that had lifted me off my feet the day before. His face showed that he was not ready for such strength from a small lady.

"That was a most interesting sermon," she said.

"I thank you very much. I—"

"Now, you mind I'm not saying it was a *great* sermon, but the ideas have distinct possibilities."

I felt I must act or Mr. Hawkes would suffer an attack of something. I planted myself between the two of them and made introductions, including in them Ms. Cromwell and Ms. Smithers. Mr. Hawkes, to save himself, called others over and introduced them in turn, so pretty soon I was kind of relegated to the outside fringe of the circle of hospitality, where I must say I was happy to be. It was like coming into the shade after having been in the glare of the sun all morning.

Debbie came around to where I was standing.

"Where've you been since Friday afternoon?" she asked. "I thought you'd be over yesterday, and we'd go to the school grounds and practice our hook shot."

I felt guilty. She would keep my secret if I told her, but it would put a lot of pressure on her, too. She would think I was doing a foolish thing which would get me in trouble. She would worry about me, and I didn't want her to worry.

"These ladies came yesterday," I said under my breath. "They're staying at our place. And you know how Dad is."

She nodded. One thing I like about Debbie is the fact that she allows me to sound off about Dad but she is still pretty fair-minded about him. She does not see him as a villain. I'm glad, because I don't think he's a villain either. He just doesn't like to work. He should have been born rich.

"Well, I'll see you in the gym tomorrow afternoon, then," she said as she moved off to join her parents. "Mr. Prima said we could have it Monday afternoons during football season."

That just about tore me up. I wasn't going to be there after school—or even *before* school. The lump that had been in my throat earlier came back and brought its cousin. I couldn't hang around that churchyard anymore.

The three ladies by that time had been not only welcomed but absorbed. Nobody seemed particularly anxious to get away from them, least of all the Reverend Mr. Hawkes. He and Ms. Smithers were all excited about old tombstones or something like that. So I told Mrs. Bendix to please tell them I had gone home to fix lunch and that they could come when they pleased.

On the way back through the cornfield I stumbled a lot because my eyes kept filling up and I couldn't always see where I was stepping.

This won't ever do, I thought. What is, is. I have to get on with my life or I will end up exactly like Dad, just drifting from job to job, sleeping late every morning and wishing that someone would give me a million dollars. By the time I got back to the house I had managed to get hold of myself.

Dad was sitting in one of the overstuffed lobby chairs reading the paper. "Well!" he said as I walked in. "How was church?"

"All right." I started upstairs to change into my jeans.

"And the ladies—are they coming back?"

"Yes, sir. They are talking to people."

"What do you think of them?" he asked, putting down the newspaper.

"Well, life surely isn't dull when they're around—you should see St. James churchyard right now!"

Dad gave a little snorting chuckle. "Yes. It's obvious that they're a bit eccentric, not to mention inveterate liars, but they're . . . well, *attractive* all the same."

I didn't like hearing him call them liars—the word was too strong. I wondered if he would think them less attractive if they were poor instead of rich, but I didn't say it.

He took up the newspaper again. "I don't think you charged them enough for their stay, considering how you put yourself out for them. And if you will recall, they paid in advance for two meals, not three."

"Don't worry about it," I said. "If they don't pay for lunch, I'll give you five dollars out of the birthday check Aunt Liddy sent me."

I escaped upstairs before he could say anything else.

By the time they returned, I had made ice tea and a large plate of sandwiches. They ate greedily, exclaiming all the while about the delightful people they had met at St. James and what a learned man the Reverend Mr. Hawkes was. They had found out more about Shad folks in two hours than I had in four years. For instance, I didn't know Mrs. Hawkes used to coach basketball, or that Mrs. Bendix' hobby was rock collecting.

Ms. Cromwell looked at her large watch, then at her two companions.

"Would you like me to bring down your . . . ah . . . bags?" Dad asked.

"In a little while," Ms. Cromwell said. "I shall call you when we're ready. We should also like to settle with you for this extra meal. Please have the bill ready."

They rose and went upstairs as though they were strung together on a single invisible thread. I watched them ascend single file and decided I needed to be up there too. I didn't want them to forget what they had promised. "Excuse me," I said to Dad. "I have to tell Ms. Nesselrode a couple of things."

The lunch dishes might not be cleared away for several days, but that wasn't my worry anymore.

The trio was in the hall whispering among themselves when I got to the top of the stairs. When they caught sight of me they stopped and looked at each other again. Then Ms. Nesselrode said in a gentle voice, "Reubella, there has been a change of plans. I don't think we'll be taking you to Raleigh this afternoon after all."

"Before you jump to conclusions we want to talk to you," Ms. Nesselrode went on. "Something unexpected has happened. You might say we are caught in a dilemma."

My insides had crumbled as soon as she said we weren't leaving. I had trusted them. How could they be so calm about double-crossing me? I didn't want to hear anything they had to say—too much time had been wasted. I'd have to hustle to make it to Raleigh before midnight.

"Forget it!" I managed to say, pushing past them to my own room. I grabbed my knapsack off the chair, stuffed my hairbrush into the side pocket, grabbed my corduroy jacket from the closet hanger, and started out. The three of them stood around the door in a close semicircle. I would have to get rough in order to get by them.

"Excuse me!" I said through clenched teeth. "I'm in a hurry."

"Reubella, you must listen to what we have to say."

"I don't have time! If I'd known you were going to back out, I'd have been in Raleigh by now, with a place to stay and everything! You just took a day out of my life!"

Ms. Cromwell advanced and, putting her hands on my shoulders, pushed me backward into the room. The other two followed and closed the door behind them.

"Now," Ms. Cromwell said, pointing to the bed, "sit there and calm yourself. I shall talk for a few minutes. At the end of that time, if you're still dead set on going to Raleigh, we will take you—this afternoon, as promised. Do you understand?"

"Why should I believe you?"

"Why, indeed?"

I sat stiffly with my arms folded across my chest, not looking at them. I made up my mind to bolt as soon as they relaxed. I didn't want any lectures on how girls my age shouldn't run away from home and how my poor father would miss me and all that junk.

"It seemed to us," said Ms. Cromwell, beginning to pace in front of me, "that you are not all that anxious to leave Shad, the town, and that you are particularly attached to this house."

"So?"

"We have devised a plan which we think will enable you to stay here."

"Look!" I said, jumping up. "I don't *need* a plan that will enable me to stay. I can stay—and rot, or starve, or live on welfare. That's what it'll be if I stay here. I'm not going to do it!"

Ms. Cromwell was unruffled. Ms. Nesselrode moved in. "How do you feel about having your cake and eating it, too?"

"I think it's not real!" I snapped.

"You could stay if you and your father had some source of steady income—"

"Sure! Or if money grew on trees or a rich uncle died and left us a million dollars. The trouble is, my dad is never going to have a steady income because he doesn't want to work."

"Reubella, we want this house."

I heard the words, but they didn't sink in. "This house? Ours? You mean . . . you want to *buy* it?"

"No—at least not for the time being. We should like to lease it and live here, with you and your father as caretakers and managers."

I sat back down on the bed, shaking my head. "I don't understand."

"For years," said Ms. Smithers, "we have been searching. Thirty-five years ago, when we met and became friends, we conceived the idea of an Old Focus Home."

"A *what?*"

"An Old Focus Home. We knew the time would come when it wouldn't be advisable for any of us to live alone. Rather than entering a nursing home or a retirement home, we hit upon the idea of pooling our resources and opening our own place. Not a *rest* home, mind you, but a place where all of our various talents and interests might be put to good use. An *un*rest home, you might say, where our lives would find their final focus and meaning."

"And for the past year we have been searching for just the right town and just the right house," Ms. Nesselrode said.

"Sometimes we would find a house that would do, but the location was bad," Ms. Cromwell added. "Or the community would seem right but there wasn't a house to be had that would accommodate our idea."

"Yes," said Ms. Smithers, "because you see, the Home wouldn't be just for the three of us, but for our friends as well. They might want to come stay for short periods of time."

"This house and this town are perfect together. We all feel that it is so—and that our meeting with you was more than fortuitous."

I didn't know what Ms. Nesselrode meant by that

word, but that was less of a puzzle to me than the idea
of the Home—my mind couldn't quite wrap itself around
such a strange notion.

"Our plan is to lease the whole house, which would
put us in charge of the premises and give us leave to do
any renovating that would be needed."

I shook my head. "Dad won't hear of it. I know he
won't."

"How about you, though—how does it strike you?"

I had to think. Running a lodge was one thing, because
the guests were so few and far between. But if the ladies
came to stay, then Dad and I would never have the house
to ourselves again. Even so, I couldn't push back the
hopeful feelings that had started poking up inside me. I
tried to be stern with myself. I didn't know a thing about
these three other than the bizarre stories they told.
Maybe they were closer to being senile than they appeared. I thought about a whole houseful of old people,
tottering around and being forgetful and fretful. I
thought about Dad's self-centeredness and his tendency
to avoid work.

"No," I said. "It wouldn't work."

Ms. Nesselrode's face fell. Ms. Cromwell turned away
and went to stand by the window. Ms. Smithers flopped
into the nearby chair and said, "Oh, heck!" Tears welled
in her eyes and spilled down her wrinkled cheeks.

That sort of shocked me. They really seemed to have
their hearts set on our place.

"Don't you understand?" I tried to soften my tone
some. "I'm fifteen years old. Any work that gets done
around here is done by me. I can't manage a rest home
—or an unrest home. You can't count on Dad to be
responsible—there's just no way."

There was a long silence. I felt tired and confused and
didn't know what I wanted. The thought of hassling my
way to Raleigh that afternoon made me want to get in a

hole and pull the dirt after me.

Suddenly Ms. Nesselrode knelt beside me and hugged me close to her. "Poor, dear child! How old you are—even older than we!"

My first impulse was to pull away, but her shoulder was solid and grandmotherly. It felt good to forget about struggling and just rest there a minute with my eyes closed.

"Reubella," said Ms. Cromwell, coming away from the window, "would you be willing to trust that we can make a go of it without making more work for you?"

"I wish I could. But I have lived with Dad a long time."

At that moment there was a tap on the door. "That's Dad, wondering whether you want your bags taken down," I said.

Ms. Smithers got up and opened the door. Dad gazed past her at the rest of us, an inquiring look on his face. "I thought perhaps you had lost track of the time—it's nearly three." He pointed at his watch.

"Yes—well. That's very kind of you." Ms. Smithers smiled sweetly.

"Mr. Foster, we'd like a word with you. Won't you come in?" Ms. Cromwell strode to the door, and although I did not actually see her put her hand on his arm and pull him into the room, it *seemed* as if that is what happened. My modest room felt shrunken to the size of a pantry.

"Will you sit?" Ms. Cromwell indicated my only chair.

"I'm sorry," said Dad. "I can't sit when so many ladies are standing. It makes me uncomfortable."

"Oh—well, in that case, we shall all sit."

The three of them sank gracefully to the floor and sat in the lotus position. Despite their ages, there wasn't a squeak of joint or crack of bone. Dad hesitated a moment, but then he sat warily—in the chair.

"What is all this—a conspiracy or something?"

"No, sir," I said. "Ms. Cromwell has a . . . a proposition."

It was strange how she could seem to be standing up pacing even when she was sitting cross-legged on the floor below Dad's eye level.

"Mr. Foster, I shall get right to the point. How would you like to have an income of twenty thousand dollars this year?"

Dad's eyes glazed. I expect mine did, too. Twenty thousand dollars! I could not even imagine how much money that was.

He cleared his throat, and when he spoke his voice was thin and dry. "What's the catch?"

Ms. Cromwell quickly explained about the Old Focus Home and how they had searched for months for the right place.

"This house and this town are the perfect combination, Mr. Foster. What we propose is that you lease us the house. Ten thousand dollars would be for the actual leasing and improvement of the property. The other ten thousand would pay your salary as manager of the Old Focus Home. If additional people have to be hired to help, we will bear that expense as well."

Dad's mouth opened and closed. Finally he managed to speak. "Manager of a nursing home? Me? You have to be kidding!" He made as though to get up.

Ms. Cromwell frowned. "Mr. Foster, it would not be a nursing home, although we certainly hope it will be a *nurturing* home!"

Dad sat back. "Ladies, I am sorry if I offended you. I didn't mean to cast aspersions. I was only thinking of my own shortcomings—I wouldn't know what to do."

"We had thought of that already," said Ms. Nesselrode. She reached into her ever-present shoulder bag and brought out a folded piece of paper. "We have written a job description. This defines the manager's duties in full.''

Dad leaned over to take the paper, but she held it just out of his reach.

"I shall read aloud," she said. "The duties of the manager of the Old Focus Home shall be as follows: Number one—to be charming to the residents and their guests, so as to help them feel that they have worth as members of humankind, even though they may be elderly and no longer producing income.

"Number two—to be responsible for recruiting and hiring qualified personnel from the local community to do whatever jobs and chores are required for the smooth running of the Home.

"Number three—to spend time contemplating the brevity of human life.''

She looked up from the paper. "That's all."

Dad rubbed his chin thoughtfully. "What's the purpose of number three?"

"That would be up to you."

There was a long silence while Dad struggled with the problem. It was always a terrible conflict for him where money and work were connected. He looked at me.

"What do you think?"

"I . . . think it's a good idea," I heard myself say.

More silence. My hands were sweaty. The Big Ben alarm clock on the nightstand clicked loudly. I looked at the hands pointing to three thirty. One thing for sure, I had missed my chance to get to Raleigh.

"On the surface it seems like a good idea," Dad said finally. "Too good, almost. It would be irresponsible of me to make a quick decision."

"I couldn't agree with you more," said Ms. Cromwell. "If you will permit us to stay another night, I'll put in a call to our attorney now and have him come down tomorrow to draw up a tentative agreement. If you like, your attorney can meet with us, too, to represent your interests."

Dad chewed his lower lip. He didn't tell the ladies he had no attorney.

"All right. The telephone is on the desk in the lobby. But remember, we're on a four-party line. You may . . . ah . . . want to phrase your conversation carefully, so as not to inform the entire town of our plan."

I thought it encouraging that he said "our plan" as though he had already made up his mind and was only holding out long enough to determine how to get the best deal for the least effort.

Our supper that night was soup and crackers. It was a subdued gathering. The weight of an unmade decision hung over us all like a limbful of snow.

"Mr. Benchley will be here shortly before noon tomorrow," Ms. Cromwell announced. "I have explained to him briefly what sort of arrangement we would be interested in."

"I will have some questions for him," said Dad. My heart sank. I was sorry Dad had so many hours to think it over. Schemes had a tendency to grow large in his imagination when he had time on his hands.

"One more thing—we would like for Reubella to be here during the negotiations," said Ms. Nesselrode. "Do you think you might write a note to her principal to excuse her from school at lunch?"

"Why does she need to be here?" Dad asked. "She's only fifteen."

"Fifteen going on thirty," Ms. Smithers said, tossing me a smile. "After all, her life will be affected by any decisions that are made. Besides that, she asks very good questions."

Dad wasn't too sold on the notion. "I realize that you

ladies have made inroads into Reubella's affections, but I certainly hope you won't use her friendship to gain some selfish ends."

I could have slid under the table. The very idea of his saying such a thing! However, Ms. Cromwell was as cool as a judge.

"Trust us," she said. Then she turned to me. "I beg your pardon for not asking if you would be willing to be here."

"Oh, sure! But I need to get back to school afterward to practice with the other girls at the gym. We're going to have a girls basketball team this year. Tryouts are in a few weeks, so we need to work hard on our day."

"Your day?"

"Yes. There's only one gym. Mr. Prima—the principal—said we could practice our shots and all in the gym on Mondays during football season. The boys usually get it the other four days."

Ms. Cromwell looked thoughtful. "I'll take you over in Buxtehude. In fact, I might even watch you practice. I have played some basketball in my day."

No more words were said about the big decision, but after the meal the ladies helped with the table-clearing and washing up. It was a sign of their desperate longing for the Yellow House. Dad was quick to note it, and smiled to himself. I couldn't help wishing they'd be more poker-faced and hard to get, for the good of all of us.

Next day at one o'clock Ms. Cromwell, wearing jodphurs and pith helmet, came for me at school in the Buxty Hooda.

"Mr. Benchley has arrived," she told me as she maneuvered the van around some school buses and out into the street. "He and your father have already begun discussing the business aspects."

"Is . . . I hope Dad is being civil," I said, looking out of the window.

"Well, I think he is doing as well as could be expected, under the circumstances."

That was not a heartening report. I decided not to ask any more questions.

The atmosphere in the dining room was as tight as twenty slingshots pulled back. I shook hands with Mr. Benchley and understood immediately why Dad might be having trouble. The lawyer was sort of a catalog person—light-blue suit pressed, little mustache neatly trimmed, handsome and smiley in a hard, lean way. Although Dad had put on his fourteen-year-old suit for the occasion, he was certainly no match in looks for Mr. Benchley. My hopes plummeted, because when Dad feels inferior, he becomes his larger-than-life actor-self to make up for it. Most people find it objectionable.

The six of us seated ourselves around the dining room table, Mr. Benchley at the head, I at the foot, and the ladies and Dad at the sides. Everyone, including the lawyer, was on the defensive. Ms. Nesselrode took charge. She cleared her throat and folded her hands upon the table in front of her. I admired how strong they looked, even when still.

"Mr. Benchley, Mr. Foster—as you know, my friends and I have been searching for some time for a home and community that would suit our various temperaments. It has been our intention, once we found such a place, to settle there and begin the next phase of our life, which is not Retirement but Commencement. A school commencement exercise launches persons into careers that use the knowledge and skills acquired up to that point. The three of us have gleaned a great deal in our combined two hundred and twenty-eight years. We want to put it to some new use, and Shad is where we should like to do it."

Ms. Cromwell nodded vigorously, murmuring "Hear! Hear!" Ms. Smithers applauded. Ms. Nesselrode inclined her head slightly.

Dad sat forward in his chair and put both hands, palms down, upon the table. "I am flattered, ladies, that you have chosen Foster Lodge as the place for your . . . er . . . Commencement. You realize, of course, that to agree to your terms will mean a drastic adjustment in life-style for Reubella and me, particularly if I am to be the manager of the Home. For that reason it will have to be worth—"

At that point Mr. Benchley made the mistake of rolling his eyes toward the ceiling and sighing, which was a dead giveaway and not lost on Dad.

"For that reason," Dad continued, this time with ice in his voice, "it must be very clear that the house and the position of manager cannot be separated. We come to-gether—the house and I. No me, no house."

He sat back and folded his arms, glaring at Mr. Bench-ley. I could only conclude that this subject had been brought up before I got there.

"I am of the opinion," Mr. Benchley said smoothly, "that we should draw up two separate contracts—one for the lease of the house and one to cover the manager's job. It seems to me that these ladies need some sort of assurance—"

"Are you implying that I could not manage the Home satisfactorily?"

"Not at all, Mr. Foster—except that you must admit you have little experience in this sort of thing."

"I am not a complete imbecile, Mr. Benchley!" Dad's face flamed. His brown hair fluffed up. "I can—"

"Gentlemen!" Ms. Cromwell's voice exploded be-tween them like a grenade. It had a quietening effect. "Let me remind you both that no one, so far as we know, has had experience managing the sort of establishment we have in mind. This may be the first of its kind in the entire world. We don't want a manager who would treat us like worn-out rag dolls. Neither do we want someone who has no interest in what we hope to do. We are of the opinion that you, Mr. Foster, are creative enough to help us make the most of our Commencement."

"Thank you," said Dad, flashing Mr. Benchley a tri-umphant look.

"Then would Mr. Foster please explain how he sees the job of manager," Mr. Benchley grumbled.

Dad took from his breast pocket the crumpled piece of paper upon which was his job description. He passed it to Mr. Benchley, who read it with a look of distaste.

"Do you find it satisfactory?" Ms. Nesselrode prod-ded.

"I find it vague, Ms. Nesselrode. And perhaps not

exacting enough. I daresay it's easy to be charming to the elderly when one is being watched, but how can you command sincerity? And as for the final requirement—contemplating the brevity of life—how can you ever satisfy yourself that the requirement is being filled?"

"We have eyes and ears, Mr. Benchley. We shall be able to tell."

Mr. Benchley leaned forward and looked her in the eye. "What if he *isn't* contemplating? What will you do then?"

It was a very good lawyer type of question I thought. Even flustering, if you were the flusterable sort. But Ms. Nesselrode was not.

"Then we shall have a talk, Mr. Benchley, and clarify things in a civilized way."

Mr. Benchley all but threw up his hands. I couldn't help feeling that he was the smartest person at the table, but it would have been disloyal for me to say so.

"What I'm saying, Ms. Nesselrode, is that in the event Mr. Foster does not work out as manager, even after you clarify things in a civilized way, you must have some legal recourse to replace him with a competent manager. Do you understand?"

Dad leaped to his feet and made a fist. "I'll sue for defamation of character! What right do you have to make such statements when you've never even seen me before today? I'm asking you to leave, Mr. Benchley. Immediately!" He pointed with a grandiose gesture toward the front door, looking for all the world like John Wilkes Booth or somebody. Mr. Benchley began stuffing papers into his briefcase. Ms. Smithers' hands fluttered at her throat. Ms. Nesselrode made little pacifying noises. Ms. Cromwell was shouting, too, but it wasn't doing any good. I banged once, loudly, on the table with the salt shaker.

"SIT DOWN!" I yelled.

It worked. They all melted back into their seats and looked at me, the ladies with some hope, Mr. Benchley with skepticism, Dad with anger.

"Now," I said, "let me say first that I think Mr. Benchley's suggestion makes perfectly good sense—there should be two contracts. Dad, if you intend to fulfill your duties to the best of your ability, you won't have any reason to worry. You *do* intend to do your best, don't you?"

"Wh-why of course I do! That's a ridiculous question, and besides, who asked you to butt in?"

That almost unnerved me, but a lot was at stake. "Dad, I don't see how you can let this chance go by. But if you do, I will tell you this—when the ladies leave, I am going with them. For good. I am tired of living like a bum."

There was a long, tense silence while he and I locked eyes. For one terrible moment I thought he was going to say "Go ahead and leave," but then he exhaled slowly and turned his palms upward.

"What can I do?" he said, looking around the table. "I know when I'm licked."

I got up and went around to where he was sitting. "I'm sorry," I mumbled, putting my arm around him. "But that's how desperate I am. I *want* to stay here, if there's something to stay for."

He nodded and patted my hand. "Two contracts," he said to Mr. Benchley in a kind of choked voice. Mr. Benchley had the grace not to gloat.

"Very well. I should have the papers ready to sign within a few days."

"I should like to say, Mr. Foster, that you are by no means 'licked,'" Ms. Nesselrode said quietly. "You could have insisted upon having your way, but lost your greatest treasure in the process. *I* think you're a very strong person."

I wanted to tell her that she was misled. I was not

Dad's greatest treasure, and if he could figure out a way to live without my usefulness, he would certainly have done it long ago. But it wouldn't do any good to say those things. As long as the ladies had confidence in him, why should I make him look bad?

Mr. Benchley finally drove away at five minutes of three, which gave me ten minutes to get back to school.

"I'll take you to the gymnasium," Ms. Cromwell said. "Give me three minutes to change."

"You look fine," I said, eyeing the jodphurs and pith helmet. "You don't have to change just to take me over to the school."

She murmured something I didn't understand because she had already disappeared upstairs before the last words were out of her mouth. I went and got into the Buxty Hooda. True to her word, she was in the driver's seat in three minutes, attired in trench coat, gray knee socks, and tennis shoes. I thought it a strange costume, but decided she was probably going to go hiking or something after she dropped me off.

"Do you think you will make the team?" she asked as we sped over bumps and swerved around corners. I held on to the armrest for dear life.

"I don't know. We've never had a girls team before —or at least not in my time. They used to have one years ago. Now they say that this year we can have a team that will play other schools in the county."

"Have you had much experience?"

"No. We've played some, in P.E. classes, but we don't get to practice in the gym very often. The boys have first claim on it."

Ms. Cromwell looked at me in a funny way. The Buxty Hooda veered slightly—we barely missed going into a ditch. "Why on earth should that be?"

"I don't know, except our boys team has always been good. They win the area championship almost every year. I guess Coach Greenlief figures they ought to have the gym most, since they have a reputation to uphold."

"How will the girls ever establish an equal reputation?"

"I suppose we have to prove ourselves."

"That's absurd! It's like applying for a job—the first question is always 'Do you have experience?' And of course, you can't have experience until someone gives you a job." She uttered a few choice words under her breath. I was surprised at her passion.

We jounced into the school grounds with a minute to spare. Ms. Cromwell drew up in front of the gym and I leaped out, yelling my thanks for the ride. A bunch of girls was sitting or standing around the entrance. Through the open door came sounds of sneakers thumping on hardwood and shouts of male voices.

"Say, what is this?" I ran up to Debbie. "I thought this was our day?"

Silence. I looked around at the faces of the other girls and saw anger, disappointment, hurt.

"We've been axed," Debbie said bitterly. "The good news came over the intercom right after you left. You may as well have stayed home."

"Been axed! What do you mean?"

"I mean there's not going to be a girls basketball team this year."

"But they can't do that! They *promised!*"

"Well, they don't know it, apparently," said Debbie, "because they've done it. And since we aren't going to have a team anyway, the boys get the gym an extra day. And there they are!" She jerked her head in the direction of the gym noises.

"I beg your pardon," said Ms. Cromwell's familiar voice behind me. "What's the problem?"

I turned. She had taken off the trench coat. There she stood, attired in the kind of outfit you only see in your grandmother's picture albums!

"It's the gym suit I wore when I coached basketball at Moriah College in 1932," she explained. "Good material. Never wears out. Now, what's all this about no girls team?"

I was immobilized, as were the other girls. The shirt was reasonable enough, but those pants! Bloomers that flared way out and gathered in at the knee. The color was mustard yellow with gray trim.

"Lordy!" Debbie said under her breath.

Ms. Cromwell waited patiently until we got an eyeful and came to our senses enough to realize she had asked a civil question. Everyone started talking at once. Finally she was able to piece the story together—the School Board, at Coach Greenlief's request, had taken back its recommendation to start a girls team. Coach Greenlief had told them he didn't have time to coach varsity and junior varsity boys' teams *and* a girls team, and that there wasn't enough practice space besides.

"Couldn't they hire another coach?" Ms. Cromwell asked.

"Not enough money." Debbie kicked at the step with her sneaker. "They said something about maybe next year."

"But that won't do *me* any good," Betty Byers said, her black face fixed in a scowl. "I'm graduating this year."

Ms. Cromwell looked at her sympathetically. Betty was obviously good material, being all of five-eleven. Beside her I feel like a pygmy, but it doesn't do you any good to be good material if you never get a chance to show what you can do.

"This is very interesting," Ms. Cromwell commented.

"Yeah, I guess." Betty tended to be on the acid side. "The way funerals and wrecks are interesting."

"No," Ms. Cromwell said firmly. "The way problems are interesting."

I realized then that no one except Debbie knew who Ms. Cromwell was. I made the introductions, explaining that she and her two friends were going to be living in Shad for a while at our house.

"I'm happy to meet all of you," Ms. Cromwell said. "I had hoped I might be able to play some basketball with you."

The eyebrows really did go up then, but she ignored that. She went over to the entrance and peered into the gym. After a moment she beckoned to me.

"Which one is the coach?" she asked.

"That older one, with the mustache."

"My goodness! He can't be more than thirty—he's a child!"

I didn't have anything to say to that. Thirty seems pretty old to me, but I suppose when you're in your seventies it does seem young.

"Well, I think I shall have to go speak to him," she said determinedly, starting to go inside.

"Ms. Cromwell, wait!" I held on to her arm.

"What?"

"Look, I . . . I don't think that's a great idea."

"Indeed? Why not?"

"Well, he doesn't like people to come in and interrupt his practice sessions with the guys. You might . . . he might get so angry that we never *could* talk him into coaching a girls team. He's kind of tough. And sometimes he has a bad temper."

Ms. Cromwell considered that a moment, then nodded. "I see your point. Another strategy is required."

"Yeah, I suppose." I didn't know what it would be. Frankly, I hadn't any hope that things could be changed. We went back over to the group.

"No need to hang around here," Betty said. "I'm going home."

"Yeah—me too," Debbie echoed. The others nodded. Those sitting on the steps got up to leave.

"Now, wait just one moment!" Ms. Cromwell's major-general voice boomed. "Here you are, all set to play basketball. So play basketball!"

I was embarrassed. "Ms. Cromwell, there's no *place* for us. The guys are in there and they aren't likely to leave any time soon."

She was looking all around, shading her eyes in order to see better. "Don't I see some goals out on the playground?"

"Yes, but that's not the same as playing in the gym on wood floors—"

"You're right. If you can play on the school ground and become really good at it, playing in the gym will be a cinch."

I could tell no one was interested, and I was casting about in my mind for some diplomatic way to get Ms. Cromwell back in the Buxty Hooda when suddenly she sprinted over to the van, slid open the rear door, and took out two basketballs. Before our eyes she headed across the gravelly playground, dribbling a ball with each hand and not missing a step. Mouths dropped open.

"Golly day—do you see that old lady?" Betty whooped. "Why, she must be ninety, and look at her dribble! I can't even do that with one ball, much less two!"

"She must've played for the Globetrotters," said Debbie. "Come on!"

We ran out to the goals, where by this time Ms. Cromwell was practicing jump shots. She dunked one after another without a miss. We lined up along the sides and watched.

Finally she stopped and looked around as though seeing us for the first time. "Oh—changed your mind, eh? O.K. Divide into teams. Here we go—you, you, you." She lined us up and divided us in about a minute, and the next thing I knew, Betty and I were jumping for the toss-up.

For the next two hours she worked our tails off. She was everywhere at once, giving pointers on dribbling, stealing the ball, shooting from the outside, hooking one from under the net. She was like a bulldozer, a lawn-mower, a streetsweeper, and a catapult combined. I wasn't conscious of anything except the game and trying to play it to suit her exacting standards.

After what seemed ages Ms. Cromwell blew the whis-tle. "Good workout, girls!" she said, a pleased look on her face. She was scarcely breathing hard, although the rest of us were ready for the dumpster.

"How . . . in . . . the . . . world . . . can . . . you . . . do . . . it?" Debbie gasped, holding her side. "I'm . . . caving in."

As for me, I could only nod, not having enough breath to speak. Ms. Cromwell looked us over. "Yes, I can see that. You aren't in shape. All right—I want you to begin running each day—possibly running to school in the morning rather than riding. You can't run very far at first if you aren't used to it, so the first day go as far as you can and then a little more. Gradually lengthen your dis-tance. You need to build up your endurance."

"How far do you run each day?" Betty asked.

"Never less than two miles, sometimes as much as six."

"Every day?"

"Haven't missed in ten years, except for the time I broke my leg skiing and had to stay in a cast five weeks. I've been getting up at four in the morning since I've been here—which reminds me. I missed this morning. I'd best be going."

"Ms. Cromwell," I said, grinning at her, "it looks like we've got us a coach."

She bounced the ball, looking down at the ground. "Well, it's up to you—"

We all burst out yelling and cheering at once, surrounding her in a huddle to give her the old rah-rah-rahrahrah, ending with CROMWELL! CROMWELL! CROMWELL! YAYYY!

"O.K.," she said, when we had calmed down. I thought she looked a little teary, but I may have been mistaken about that. "I expect you can't have official practices until the season begins—that's a rule in most schools. But I see no reason why you can't work out in the afternoons to get ready for tryouts. I'll be here tomorrow to sort of give you some pointers."

It ended up that every one of us piled into the Buxty Hooda, and by the time the last person had been delivered to her own front porch, Ms. Cromwell was a solid heroine. Debbie was the last to get out.

"One thing for sure, if we do have our own team, I want our uniforms to look just like yours," she said to Ms. Cromwell. "It'll fake everyone out. They'll be laughing so hard they'll neglect to notice how tough we are, and—*pow!*"

Ms. Cromwell and I laughed all the way home.

That evening we finished dinner in high spirits. I was glad Dad didn't seem to be mad at me for making him look bad in front of Mr. Benchley. Afterward we sat on the screened porch in the twilight. Ms. Cromwell peered through binoculars at the lights of boats winking on the river. In the half-dark Ms. Smithers sketched the river and the black trees standing out from the skyline on the far shore. Ms. Nesselrode sat with her hands folded peacefully in her lap and a contented smile on her face. Dad smoked his pipe and told river stories as though he had lived in this place all his life.

As for me, I sat in the porch swing and hugged myself. If I'd had some champagne, I would have proposed a toast. Having the three ladies settle in with us felt solid, permanent, and warm—just like when I was little and was sitting tightly sandwiched between Dad and my mother on the front seat of the car, or holding a hand of each of them as we walked in the park.

I suppose I had taken for granted way back then that my life was always going to be warm and snug, but somewhere along I discovered that it is hardly ever like that. Probably it wouldn't be that way with the ladies either. I shivered.

"Cold?" Dad asked. "I'll go get you a sweater if you are."

I shook my head. It had been ages since he asked me how I felt or if I wanted anything. "Thanks anyway," I said. If his intentions were good, I surely didn't want to discourage him.

"The river is well named—Peaceful," Ms. Smithers said, laying aside her sketch pad and pencil.

Ms. Nesselrode nodded. "I am reminded of a poem by the French writer, Paul Bourget. It is called 'Beau Soir.' " She began to speak French, which I do not understand. Her voice rose and fell like a mild wind blowing, or like a word song without music.

"That's very lovely," Dad said quietly when she had finished. "What do the words mean?"

Ms. Nesselrode hesitated. "Some people might think the words are sad, but I find them comforting, nevertheless. I suppose a rough translation would be something like this:

> "When in the setting sun
> the streams glow red
> and a slight chill settles over the fields,
> a charge to be glad seems to emanate
> from everything,
> and rises to the troubled heart.
> A charge to taste the delight of being alive
> while one is young and the evening is fair;
> for we shall move on
> just as that stream does . . .
> It goes to the sea,
> we to the grave."

Dad got up from his chair and went to stand at the edge of the porch with his back to us, his forehead pressed against the screen. I went to stand beside him. In the dying light his face was sad. He put an arm over my shoulder and gestured with his pipe toward the river.

"Look at all those waves," he said, trying to be jovial, but it wasn't working. "All heading for the sea—achieving their destiny without having to do anything but continue in the same direction."

"That's where people and waves are different," I said. "People have to do something besides move forward between being born and dying. Otherwise, what's the point?"

"Good question," Dad mumbled. "What, indeed?"

We stood there for several minutes, until the glow had disappeared from the sky. When we turned, the three ladies were no longer there.

Since nothing was legal until Mr. Benchley's papers were drawn up and signed, the three ladies were for the time being guests in the Foster Lodge and Tourist Home. Dad and I prepared and served meals, changed the bed linens, and put out little soaps the way we always did for Lodge guests. That part was tiresome and time-consuming, mostly because neither of us was used to perpetual customers. But I will say that Dad assumed more than his usual share of the chores.

On nice evenings we would sit out on the screened porch and talk. One of those nights the ladies learned about Dad's having been orphaned at an early age and having to make it pretty much on his own.

"You must have been very lonely sometimes, without any family," Ms. Nesselrode said softly.

Dad shrugged. "I never thought about it much. My Aunt Liddy was enough family—nearly worked me to death keeping me grateful to her for not packing me off to a children's home. Sometimes I wish she'd done it."

He wouldn't talk about it any more. I knew he didn't like Aunt Liddy much, but since she sent me a check every birthday I had never troubled myself to find out why. Now I saw him in a somewhat different light and his attitude was a little more understandable.

While I did my homework, Dad and the ladies went over their plans for the Home, like little children playing a favorite game. The walls of the house were knocked out, replaced, and redecorated a dozen different ways. Ms. Cromwell devised an activity chart for prospective residents and guests that included recreation, crafts, lectures, athletic programs, philosophy courses, yoga, oil-painting instruction, music, and community service projects. Ms. Smithers planned a visitation program for Shad's senior citizens. Ms. Nesselrode spoke of organizing a community orchestra and chorus. It was too visionary for me. I tend to bog down on more practical points, such as who is going to clean the johns every day.

Mr. Benchley was back on Saturday with his briefcase and papers. This time Dad behaved better. He was even civil to the lawyer. We all went over the contracts, but I was the only person present who did not get to sign anything. That is the problem with being a minor.

Something happened next day that brought home to me once and for all the fact that our new residents were not just ordinary people. We went to the Methodist Church this time. A lot of the same people were there who had been at the Episcopal Church the week before, because Shad folks go wherever there is preaching, regardless of the denomination. Mr. Fergus, the minister, is a short, swarthy person who tells stories about people who have been converted. He knows more conversion stories than anyone I have ever seen. I have wondered sometimes whether he made them up, but he always tells them as though he knew the people personally, and you don't want to go up to a preacher and ask him outright if he is telling the truth.

Afterward, when the congregation gathered to talk in the churchyard, it was clear that the three ladies had been welcomed and claimed by Shad. No one gave them funny looks anymore. Word had gotten around that Ms.

Cromwell was helping us with basketball, so a number of parents came over to thank her. Unbeknown to me, Ms. Smithers had spent most of the week visiting up and down the town. As a result, she knew almost as many people by name as I did, and was kept busy introducing Ms. Nesselrode and Ms. Cromwell to her newfound friends.

The pianist at the Methodist Church, Miss Preddy, was a shy person who lived with her mother. In a crowd of people she seemed to become transparent, so that even though she was there and you could see her, you were really seeing through or over or around her. She almost never spoke to anyone unless they asked her a direct question. I was amazed when she edged up to Ms. Nesselrode on the church steps and whispered,

"Are you *really* Hollis Nesselrode?"

"Why, yes! And who might you be?"

"I . . . I'm JoAnne Preddy." Miss Preddy stuck out her thin hand and Ms. Nesselrode took it more gently than she usually does. "All my life I thought Hollis Nesselrode was a man—I just admire your compositions tremendously! I played your 'Étude in E Flat for the Left Hand' in my senior recital in college."

I suppose my eyes were about twice their normal size. Even though I'd heard Ms. Smithers and Ms. Cromwell talk about their friend's distinguished musical career, I guess I hadn't really believed it.

Ms. Nesselrode's eyes filled with tears. "How very kind of you, my dear! And how nice to be admired by someone as talented as you—I was greatly impressed by your playing this morning!"

I thought Miss Preddy was going to faint. She turned red, then white, and her breath came in little spasms. "Oh, thank you!" she whispered. Then, because it was too much for her, she hastened down the steps and vanished like smoke.

"Good grief!" I exclaimed. "I never in my life heard her say that many words at one time. Are you really famous?"

But Ms. Nesselrode ignored my question. "H'mmm. The girl needs to know how good she is. Anyone who performs the Left Hand Étude has to be an accomplished pianist. Perhaps, when my piano comes—" And she turned to speak to someone else.

I mulled over this as we walked home. It had seemed more comfortable somehow to believe that our new residents were eccentric old ladies given to fabricating exciting stories of their lives. If they really *were* great and famous, they might expect things . . .

Knowing the carpenters were coming to renovate did not prepare me for the overnight change. When I came home Monday afternoon hungry as three bears, everything in the house was covered with a fine film of sawdust and plaster. Some walls had been knocked out, leaving great gaping holes between rooms. A couple of windows had been boarded over. I could scarcely recognize the house as the same place I had left only that morning. Furthermore, the Foster Lodge and Tourist Home sign had been taken down, and in its place hung a bright yellow-and-black sign reading THE OLD FOCUS HOME OF SHAD, INC.

I found the old sign leaning against a wall in the lobby and asked Dad if I might keep it in my room.

"Sure—do what you like with it. I can't imagine you wanting the old rotten thing."

I took it upstairs to my room and leaned it against the chair. Then I sat on the edge of the bed and gazed at it. I never in a million years thought that I would feel sad about the end of Foster Lodge, but there I was with a lump in my throat. The letters on the sign wavered and blurred. I blinked, blew my nose, and turned the sign to the wall so I couldn't see it anymore.

Thereafter the dust and plaster became part of our life, thicker with each passing day. It got so that I felt I would do almost anything to keep from going home in the afternoon. There wasn't a single orderly place where a person could get herself together. Maintaining the house was a discouraging job.

There were other changes, too, which were harder to deal with than plaster dust. Dad and the three ladies still went over their plans every evening, but the tone of their conversations had changed. It was no longer fun and games, but deadly serious. They argued a lot.

Each of the women had put in for some special sort of room—Ms. Nesselrode had requested a music room for her piano and phonograph. Ms. Cromwell had asked for a large area with glassed-in shelves around the walls for her various nature collections and athletic trophies. Ms. Smithers insisted on a sunny room with extra windows on the first floor for her painting and sculpting. Dad wanted all the rooms to be less specialized, in the event they had to be used for other purposes in later years. The arguments almost always ended at the same impasse, because, after all, it was the ladies' money that was making the renovations possible, but it was Dad's house. Sometimes, in the heat of the fray, I would simply pick up my books and go out on the porch by myself, even though the nights had begun to be chilly. Most of the time Dad and the ladies didn't notice that I had left.

I was not the only one affected by the changes. Ms. Cromwell did a lot of pacing and talking in a loud voice. She also increased the number of miles she ran each day. Ms. Nesselrode was restless, wandering from room to room and making suggestions to the carpenters, until Dad finally asked her to find some other way to employ her pent-up energy. Ms. Smithers had a tendency to com-

plain—the food wasn't cooked just right, or she had
heard Ms. Cromwell snoring through the walls and
hadn't been able to sleep, or the dust was getting into her
oil paintings before they could dry properly. Dad virtually stopped eating and went about with a perpetual
frown.

Just when I thought I couldn't stand another day of it,
the hammering and sawing stopped, the final dust settled,
the painters came and went, a crew of men and women
recruited by Dad cleaned the place from attic to base-
ment, and there was the Old Focus Home, ready to
receive.

It was gorgeous. The walls were white or papered with
bright-colored prints. The ladies had insisted on keeping
the old carpeting in the halls and on the stairs, but new
rugs had been put down in all ten upstairs rooms, including mine. I wandered in and out of them, smelling the
fresh paint and admiring the furnishings and marveling
that this was my very own home. It was going to be great
to have my friends over for slumber parties and wiener
roasts—I'd never had the courage to ask them before,
there not being extra money for potato chips and other
snacky things.

For the first time in many days, the dinner hour was
peaceful. The five of us beamed at each other and admired the house all over again.

"The moving van should come any day now," Ms.
Smithers said.

Dad's eyebrows climbed. "I thought you brought all
your worldly goods in the van."

"Actually," said Ms. Nesselrode, "we did bring most
of them. But there were a few items that wouldn't fit—
my Steinway, for instance."

"But you mustn't be worried," Ms. Cromwell said
hastily. "We don't have a great deal. Just a few things that

will make us feel more completely at home."

"Oh, I shall be so *happy* to have my piano again!" Ms. Nesselrode's face shone. "I've missed it terribly."

"Yes—and my rock collection," Ms. Cromwell said dreamily. "It hasn't been out of the crates since I retired from the museum. It will look wonderful in those glass cupboards."

"Well, you will laugh at me, I'm sure," said Ms. Smithers, "but the thing that I've missed most of all is my life-size statue of Robert E. Lee. It always stood by the door . . ."

Her voice trailed away. Nobody laughed.

"I hope," said Dad in the silence, "that the place won't seem too cluttered."

"I don't think it will at all," Ms. Nesselrode assured him, "and these little familiar touches will mean so much to our friends when they come to the dedication ceremony—"

"Dedication ceremony! *What* dedication ceremony?"

Dad's explosive reaction took the ladies by surprise.

"Why—we *have* to have a dedication ceremony, Mr. Foster!" Ms. Smithers said. "It wouldn't be right to begin the Home without a proper ceremony."

"We've planned it for the weekend following Thanksgiving," said Ms. Cromwell, consulting her calendar watch. "That will give us time to get the Home into smooth working condition. We—"

"Don't you think," Dad interrupted, "that as manager of the Home I should have been informed of this?"

An uneasy silence followed his question. The peacefulness in the atmosphere had definitely thinned. I sighed. We were off again!

"All right." Dad spoke deliberately. "We must have an understanding from the start. If I am going to be manager of this . . . this establishment, then I have to know when you plan to have guests—or ceremonies, as the case may be."

Ms. Nesselrode sighed. "I suppose you're right. But it takes all the spontaneity out of things, don't you think?"

"My dear Ms. Nesselrode, *some* things require planning ahead."

"Do you object to a dedication ceremony?"

"I don't see how I can object, if that is what you want. But a thing like that calls for a great deal of advance preparation. I mean, the town dignitaries will have to know about it, to put it on their calendars—"

"I've already seen to that." Ms. Smithers beamed. "Mr. Fergus, Mr. Hawkes, and Mr. Chrismon are the clergy who will participate."

"And the mayor and the town council," said Ms. Nesselrode.

"And the governor," Ms. Smithers finished.

"The governor!" Dad yelped.

"Yes, of course. He's the son of one of my dearest friends. He used to play on my front porch."

For a moment Dad was speechless. He had become very pale. Probably he was thinking that if the governor was coming, he would have to buy a new suit. When he finally spoke, his voice sounded thin.

"Would you mind telling me—if it's not too much trouble—just how many people are coming to this affair?"

"Well, we're inviting several of our special, intimate friends to stay here in the Home over the Thanksgiving holiday," Ms. Nesselrode said. "We're sending invitations for the day to about one hundred out-of-town guests. And of course, everyone *in* town is invited. After all, the Home really belongs to Shad. We plan a large reception after the ceremony, with punch and cookies and peanuts—and a tour of the facilities."

"I see. And which of you is going to do all the work?"

The three ladies looked at him. "We haven't really worked out those details yet."

Dad put his head in his hands. "Tell me I'm dreaming."

"You're dreaming," Ms. Smithers said agreeably. "There. Does that help?"

I had stayed out of it up to this point, but I was beginning to feel sorry for Dad. After all, he was taking his job seriously, and I was afraid that if they gave him too much to worry about at first, he would throw in the towel.

"I think it would be a good idea if you would write down for Dad everything you've planned," I said. "The invitation list and all. He's going to have to hire extra help to begin getting ready."

"Yes, that's reasonable," Ms. Nesselrode agreed. "I shall write it out for you this very evening, Mr. Foster."

After dinner the ladies went up to their rooms instead of staying in the lobby to talk. I tried to settle on the couch and read, but I couldn't concentrate. Dad looked discouraged and worried. He sat in his chair and stared into space.

"It'll be O.K.," I told him. "With the extra help, everything will go as smooth as silk."

"Reubella, I don't know whether I can do what they expect."

It was a stark statement, probably as honest as he had ever made in my presence.

"Well," I said, swallowing hard, "you didn't spend all those years on the stage for nothing. You can certainly *act* like you know what you're doing."

A grin spread over his face. He got up and came over to the couch. "Reubella, what did I do to deserve a daughter like you?"

"Something bad, probably," I said. "But I hope you don't have to pay for it the rest of your days."

He shook his head, tousling my hair the way he used to when I was a little girl. "That's not what I meant, young'un."

He didn't elaborate and I didn't ask him to. At least he still considered me useful.

The noise of an engine roaring in the driveway woke me up the next morning, but since my room was on the river side of the house I had no idea what was going on. I jumped out of bed, pulled on jeans and shirt, and raced downstairs. Dad was standing sleepy-eyed in the lobby, his hair mussed and his old bathrobe half tied, peering through the window. He was muttering choice words under his breath. I missed most of them, but got a few snatches, such as ". . . this ungodly hour" and ". . . indecent time of day."

"What is it?" I rubbed at the sleep in my eyes. "Somebody get the wrong house?"

"It's the moving van." He rubbed his scalp with both hands as if he expected that to help him think better. It only made his hair stand on end more than ever. "Why couldn't they have waited another hour? It's only six o'clock, for God's sake!"

Heavy footsteps sounded on the porch. Dad opened the door before the person they belonged to could knock.

The man was huge and did not look as though he were any too happy about being up at such an hour either.

"This the . . . uh . . ." He consulted the yellow piece

of paper in his hand. "Old Focus Home?"

Dad nodded. "Yes, it is."

The man looked at him hard for a moment, frowning. "You don't look so old."

"I'm the manager." Dad drew himself up and looked as dignified as he could, tattered bathrobe and all.

"I brought some stuff down from Raleigh," the man said. "Me and my crew are ready to move it in. Where you want it?"

"Frankly, I don't know. I suppose you can begin by putting it here in the lobby while I go wake up the residents and get them down here to sort out what belongs to them."

The man looked past Dad and shook his head. "This stuff ain't gonna fit in no lobby," he said positively. "And my crew ain't gonna want to move it twice. Our contract says we place it as we bring it in. Period."

Dad and I looked at each other. "Go wake them up, Reubella. Tell them to get down here as quickly as they can."

An hour later the Old Focus Home was about as unfocused as it could possibly be, with the three old ladies in nightgowns and robes, their hair flying about, directing the movers first here, then there with their precious belongings.

There were crates of rocks and shells which Ms. Cromwell had collected from all over the world. There were enough books to start a library. I saw—among other things—scuba diving equipment, a life-size marble statue of Robert E. Lee, easels and canvases, large paintings in gilt frames, a sewing machine, water skis, and an ancient typewriter. When the men started bringing in Ms. Nesselrode's famous Steinway—the one in which she had smuggled the documents from Norway—she was all aflutter, urging them not to drop it and to be extra careful, until one moving man sputtered at her that if she'd get out of the way and be quiet, they would do just fine!

At that point I withdrew to the kitchen and made my solitary breakfast. For once in my life I was glad I had someplace to go, even if it had to be school.

The Home was still in an uproar when I departed for school. Dad gave me a pathetic look as I kissed him good-by and ran out. But by the time I returned home in the afternoon everything was in place. Thanks to Ms. Smithers, the townspeople had come to the rescue, finishing up the work the movers had left undone. The easels and paintings were in Ms. Smithers' studio. The rocks, shells, and books had been arranged in the glass cabinets and cupboards. Ms. Nesselrode's Steinway had come to rest at last in the music room, unharmed. The piano tuner from Ferris was working on it at that very moment.

"Where's Dad?" I asked Ms. Cromwell, not seeing any signs of him anywhere.

She frowned slightly. "I believe he retired to his room after lunch and asked not to be disturbed until dinner. Your father ought to get more exercise, Reubella. He's not in shape."

Probably I am naive, or maybe I just expect more of adults than they are able to deliver, but I was sure that at last things would calm down and that life would become routine and peaceful. However, I reckoned without the consequences of the arrival of the piano.

I had thought Ms. Cromwell was a disciplined person, with all her running in every kind of weather and her insistence that we girls do the same, but it soon became apparent that Ms. Nesselrode's devotion to the piano was like nothing I had ever seen before. Early the first morning she got up, ate breakfast, and immediately went to the instrument. She practiced scales and other finger exercises. She was at it when I left for school. When I came home in the afternoon, I heard the notes when I was still several houses away.

At first I was fascinated, because I had never seen a person do such acrobatics on a piano, except on television. Her fingers moved so fast they were a blur in the mirror behind the keyboard. Sometimes her whole arm blurred. I could see why she was so strong—you really have to have arm muscles to play that way!

But after two days of it, I began to have headaches. Instead of studying or reading, I would find myself listening to her play. My mind swarmed with the melodies of the pieces she happened to be practicing. At night, when everything was quiet at last, it seemed as though I could still hear her playing—even in my dreams. The final straw came when I flunked an algebra test for the first time, simply because I hadn't been able to concentrate on my studying the night before.

I couldn't face going home in my disrupted state of mind, especially when the sounds of the piano drifted to meet me before I got to our street. I began to entertain rash notions of hitchhiking to Ferris, never to return.

So instead of turning in at our place, I kept going in the direction of Prebble's Point, which is my thinking place. Something had to be done, but I had to figure out what my rights were in the matter. After all, with the ladies paying for everything, maybe Dad and I didn't have any rights anymore.

It was a cool, gray day. The wind blowing off the river was sharp and smelled of wet boards and marsh grass. I climbed down the bluff to the shoreline and found a seat at one end of a rotten tree trunk that had fallen partly into the river. The bluff broke the wind's force so that I wasn't too cold. I sat for a long time and watched the small whitecaps on the waves. Gradually the sounds of the water and wind displaced the sounds of Ms. Nesselrode's piano, and I began to feel almost human again.

I don't know what made me look up, because with the river noises and the wind in my ears I certainly didn't hear anything, but I happened to glance over my shoulder and saw Ms. Smithers standing at the top of the bluff in her purple jump suit. She was hugging her fur coat close to her. She must have been standing there for some time looking at me, because as soon as I saw her, she waved.

By now it must be said that the purple jump suit and the red satin dress were her two costumes, other than the caftan she wore around the house. The coat was a relic of her past. She had told me she kept it for sentimental reasons despite its moth-eaten appearance. It had been given to her by an Italian viscount. "He had no use for it," she had said. "It was very hot in the part of Italy where he lived."

"I hope you don't mind," she said now, scrambling down the bluff. "I saw you head this way a little while ago and decided to join you."

I moved over and gave her room on the log. Thinking she might be in a talkative mood, I braced myself to listen, but such was not the case. She looked at the river and sighed occasionally, but for a long time she said nothing.

"Holly's playing gets on my nerves," she blurted suddenly.

I stared, astonished.

"It isn't just her playing," she said hastily, noting my expression. "I've never been able to tolerate *any* piano-playing for long periods of time."

"B-but you knew that if the three of you lived together, you'd have to hear her play," I said, thinking how dumb I had been to assume I was the only one bothered.

She sighed again and tossed a piece of driftwood into the river. "Yes, but the reality of it didn't hit me until these past two days. It would be awfully nice if playing the piano were as quiet as painting with oils." She shivered and drew the mangy fur a bit closer. "I don't suppose you mind at all?"

"Sometimes." I tossed a pebble as hard as I could. It did not seem wise to reveal the extent of my feelings.

"Well, I suppose there's no help for it. We knew from the beginning that we were very different and had habits that would annoy each other. But we didn't see that as a terrible problem so long as we each had a place of our own to which we could retreat." Her face frowned into a hundred tiny wrinkles. "The trouble is, one cannot retreat from the sound of the piano unless one comes all the way down here. And it's too cold."

I had a vision of the whole town retreating from the sound of Ms. Nesselrode's piano, leaving her surrounded by a wide, lonely emptiness. It made me sad. What was the good of doing what you loved if it drove away all the people you loved?

"You have to tell her," I said with great firmness. "One thing about a whole lot of people living together —kin or not—you have to tell each other what is bothersome."

"You're right, of course," she said, looking at me so intently that I began to feel guilty. "But it's terribly hard. Risky. Suppose they don't love you any more? Suppose their feelings are hurt beyond repair?"

"Maybe Ms. Cromwell could help."

"I don't know. Most of the time when Holly is playing, Connie is nowhere around. I rather think I shall have to handle this by myself, since I am the complainant."

I could not bring myself to admit that I, too, was a complainant. It would be so much better if the ladies could settle it among themselves and I could stay out of it, except maybe to say encouraging things on Ms. Smithers' side of the argument. However, I knew that she was the most timid of the three, despite her flashy clothes. Conflict of any sort made her squint her eyes and try to disappear.

"I—I hope you are able to settle it to your satisfaction," I said. We got up from the damp log and climbed the bank to go home.

"Yes. So do I." Her voice was sad. "Holly and Connie are all I've got now."

Except for my own tension brought on by wondering what Ms. Smithers would do, dinner that evening was about as usual. Ms. Cromwell had been devoting her energies to organizing the Episcopal women into a track team, with Mrs. Hawkes as assistant coach. She was full of plans for them to enter the Masters Tournament the following year. Dad spoke of hiring a secretary to handle the correspondence about the dedication ceremony. I darted a glance at Ms. Smithers. She was pushing her food about on her plate in a distracted manner. It would be only a matter of time before Ms. Cromwell noticed and commented. That would unnerve Ms. Smithers, who would then be thrown into a state of confusion. I debated tossing a tiny piece of potato at her, just as a reminder.

"I'm composing a most exciting work," Ms. Nesselrode said, beaming at each of us. "I believe it may be unique. It feels quite different from anything I've ever written—or heard, for that matter."

Ms. Smithers looked up from pushing her food about. She had a hopeful expression in her eyes.

"I have even let myself think," Ms. Nesselrode went on, "that the North Carolina Symphony might be interested in giving the premiere performance. It's a sort of concerto, but not quite. In addition to the orchestra, we would need a chorus—and soloists, both vocal and instrumental."

"My goodness, Holly—are you trying to write another *Messiah*?" Ms. Cromwell asked.

"Oh, it will be much grander than *that*," she answered modestly. "I'm calling it *The New Symphonic Concertora-*

torio . . . in C sharp. I believe that if I continue with my practice, I shall be able to perform the piano solo myself."

"That . . . brings up something I'd like to . . . discuss," Ms. Smithers said breathlessly. All eyes turned in her direction. Her face seemed to become less distinct, as though suddenly she had forgotten what she intended to say.

"You—you were speaking of 'grand' and that made me think—made me think—what I mean is, your grand piano is . . . is . . ."

"Is my playing the piano bothering you, Ernestine?"

Ms. Smithers nodded, looking at Ms. Nesselrode with eyes that begged forgiveness but didn't really expect to get it.

"I see." The light left Ms. Nesselrode's face.

Ms. Cromwell looked back and forth at them warily, as though she could not make up her mind whose side to take. I could appreciate her dilemma. Dad excused himself from the table, saying he had to make a phone call.

"It's not your fault, Holly," Ms. Smithers said miserably. "You remember that Walker used to play the piano constantly—he was quite good at it. He played when I wanted to talk or go to the theater or tell him what I had done during the day. It was his way of getting away from me. Hearing the music makes all of those old, bad feelings come back."

Ms. Nesselrode's face cleared dramatically. "Of course! I should have remembered, Ernestine. How thoughtless of me!"

"Oh, no—you aren't thoughtless. I didn't know it would bother me. After all, this is the first time we've really lived together. Up to now we only talked about it."

"Well, there's nothing to do but stop the piano-playing. I can't bear the thought of your suffering day after day."

"No! You can't give it up," Ms. Smithers countered with equal firmness. "I'd leave before I'd let you do that."

They haggled over who would make the sacrifice, with Ms. Cromwell looking more and more desperate in her neutrality. I sat where I was, pinching my bread into little doughy pills and wondering what to do. Walker must have been Ms. Smithers' husband. Funny she had never mentioned him before. I thought again about the town retreating from the sound of the piano, leaving Ms. Nesselrode alone. If only there was a way to contain the sound—

"Say—that's *it!*" I jumped up, bumping the table and knocking over a water glass, the contents of which fell into Ms. Cromwell's lap.

"Heavens, Reubella—do be careful!" She dabbed at her lap with her napkin while Ms. Smithers attempted to soak up the spilled water with the overhang of the table-cloth. For the next few moments, everyone forgot the argument. Then Ms. Smithers suddenly remembered and turned to me.

"*What's* it?"

"I was just going to say that no one has to give up anything. You can soundproof the music room, like the radio stations do their studios. Ms. Nesselrode can play twenty-four hours a day and no one will ever know."

The three of them looked at me, dumbfounded.

"Reubella," said Ms. Smithers, "you're a genius!"

"Yes, you are," Ms. Nesselrode said fervently. "An absolute genius. It's the perfect solution. I shall pay for the soundproofing. I can have pupils come in for lessons."

"*I* shall pay for the soundproofing," Ms. Smithers said. "I was the one who complained."

"Only because you're more honest than most," Ms. Nesselrode answered. And they were off again, arguing about who would pay for the soundproofing. I clutched my head.

"Girls!" Ms. Cromwell asserted herself at last. "You will each pay half the cost. End of argument."

There was a brief, stunned silence. Then all three broke into relieved chatter.

"Aren't we silly?" Ms. Nesselrode wiped at her eyes. "The solution is so simple, and yet we stew about like . . . like—"

"—like lobsters in a pot of hot water," Ms. Cromwell finished. "It's a good thing we have someone objective and sensible like Reubella around to set us straight."

They all smiled at me. I did not feel particularly victorious, since I was probably the least objective of all and had been too cowardly to say so.

Dad came back to the table in time for dessert and was informed of the solution, which he heartily approved. All was merry again—at least for everyone but me. The crisis among them had been like a near-drowning, and had left me feeling uncertain again about their stability. The thought that I might have to come up with solutions to their problems on a regular basis made me tired all the way to my marrow.

8

Third-period social studies class had just gotten under way when Mr. Prima's voice came over the intercom.

"Ms. Hedwick, would you please send Reubella Foster to the office?"

You could have knocked me over. I had never been called to the office in my entire school career. The other people in class were as surprised as I was, but that didn't keep them from cracking the usual jokes about how I'd been caught at last, or I should've known better than to smoke in the girls' bathroom.

"What do you suppose it is?" Debbie whispered as I got up to leave.

"Search me! I haven't done anything."

I went down the long hall to Mr. Prima's office, not scared, because I didn't have anything to be scared about, but plenty curious.

"Hello, Reubella," Mrs. Kalley, the secretary, greeted me. "Sit there and Mr. Prima will be with you as soon as he finishes making a phone call."

She didn't seem to be expecting anything drastic to happen, so why should I? I sat on the long bench by the door and looked around at all the stuff on the walls—

career posters and notices to teachers, some student art work, and a framed platitude or two. Fortunately, I didn't have to sit long. It would have been a boring wait.

Mr. Prima came to the door and beckoned me in. He is a middle-aged person with blond hair and a face shaped like the moon. His eyes are too close together for the width of his face, but he can't help that any more than I can help being tall. He looked at me over the tops of his glasses and smiled pleasantly. I smiled back, to let him know I wasn't scared.

"Sit down, Reubella." He pointed to a chair and I sat in it, feeling like I was in a doctor's office and was about to be told I had lice or something annoying but not serious. The chair was hard. The arms of it were too far apart to support my elbows.

"I understand," he began, "that you weren't at school the day I announced there would be no girls basketball team this year."

"Yes, sir. But I sure found out about it when I came back that afternoon!"

"H'mmm. Yes. Well, as I explained to the others, the School Board made the decision based on Coach Greenlief's recommendation. He doesn't have time to work with the girls this year—you know his schedule."

"Yes, sir."

"I understand that the girls have been practicing nonetheless."

Something in his tone made warning flags go up in my brain. "Well, I don't know that you could call it practice," I said, "since we don't have a team. We just go out on the playground and shoot baskets and all."

We looked at each other.

"Just you girls?"

"Yes—and Ms. Cromwell. She's a lady who is staying at our house."

Mr. Prima leaned forward like a fisherman whose cork

has just gone under. "This Ms. Cromwell—I believe I heard that she has volunteered to coach the girls team?"

"Yes, sir! She's already—"

"I see. Well, Reubella, I'm afraid I'll have to call a halt to any after-school basketball for the girls—in the light of the School Board's ruling, that is."

My head buzzed as I tried to make some sense of what he was saying. That was difficult, since it made absolutely no sense at all.

"Mr. Prima, did the Board make the ruling because there was no coach for us?"

"Essentially." He nodded and turned a red pencil over and over in his hand. "That, and no place to practice."

"So if we had a coach and a place to practice—and it didn't interfere with the boys or cost anyone any money —it would probably be all right for us to have a team?"

"I really couldn't say."

"But probably?"

"Reubella, I can't answer that. All I can say now is that any practicing you girls do after school is an unauthorized activity. We can't have it because our insurance doesn't cover unauthorized activities. If one of you got hurt—"

"Well, why don't you just authorize it, then? Ms. Cromwell has volunteered to be our coach, and she's an expert—used to coach at Moriah College." I didn't mention what year. "We can keep on practicing on the school grounds in the afternoons. We won't get in anyone's way, and—"

"Reubella, I'm not in a position to make that decision. I'm sure your Ms. Cromwell is a fine person and all that, but these things have to go through proper channels."

My temper was building to the boiling point and I did not know whether I would be able to hold it in. I counted my fingers and took a couple of deep breaths.

"Ms. Cromwell is a very famous woman," I said, not knowing if I stretched the truth. "She is known worldwide for her nature lectures. We are terribly lucky to have her in Shad."

Mr. Prima frowned. "Is that so? What's she doing in Shad, then?"

The unspoken part of his question was "if she's all that great." I debated telling him something about the Old Focus Home but decided he didn't have the imagination to handle it.

"She and some friends like it here," I said lamely.

"Ms. Cromwell should have come to me first and told me what she wanted to do," Mr. Prima said self-righteously. "I shall have to insist that you girls stop practices until this is all straightened out and approved. Otherwise you risk being suspended for breaking the rules."

"But, Mr. Prima, it isn't fair! We aren't bothering anyone—"

"Reubella, I'm not going to argue with you about this. You are a sensible girl and have never caused any trouble, and I know you won't now. We shall try to get back to the Board and perhaps make a new recommendation." He didn't say it with any conviction.

"When does the Board meet again?"

"After Halloween."

"But that's too late!" I rose up out of the chair. "We'll lose weeks of practice and won't be able to get on the schedules of the other schools!"

Mr. Prima lifted his shoulders slightly. "Well, that's the way it is. I'm sorry." He looked at his watch. "I expect you'd better go back to social studies now."

It would have been a crime to burst out screaming right there in front of him, so I held on until I could get out of Mrs. Kalley's sight and down the hall to the bathroom. No one else was there. I turned on three of the faucets full force and then told the bare walls what I thought of Mr. Prima and the School Board in no uncertain terms.

When the bell rang to change classes, I was in no condition to leave. Debbie came in, took one look, and dropped her books on the floor.

"Reubella, what in the world!"

"I'm so mad I can't see straight! I'm afraid if I go out there, I'll kill somebody!"

Just then Betty Byers and Dorinda Marsh came in, along with a couple of other girls who had been practicing with us. I told them what Mr. Prima had said. One by one they went up in smoke.

Fortunately, Debbie is a level-headed person. "O.K., we've got to play by the book or we'll lose everything," she said firmly. "We're all going to our classes now, and we're not going to open our mouths about this thing—to *any*one. Understand?"

"But where does that get us?" Betty stormed. "Be good, sweet little girls, and you'll all go to heaven when you die!"

"Reubella is going to make a phone call at lunch period," Debbie said. "She's going to tell Ms. Cromwell what's up, and Ms. Cromwell will no doubt get over here faster than a speeding bullet. She can handle Mr. Prima and the Board and Mr. Greenlief with one hand tied behind her back—if we don't mess things up for her before she has a chance."

Debbie was right, of course. We left the john, vowing to keep our mouths shut, and headed for class.

The only telephone in school is in the office, and we're not supposed to use it unless there is an emergency, such as an earache or cramps or something like that. Even when you get to use it, you don't have any privacy—anyone who happens to be within earshot can hear what you say. I reminded Debbie of that. She thought a moment.

"All right, here's what we'll do. You and Betty and I will go to the office during lunch period because you have forgotten to bring your lunch money to school and you have to get Ms. Cromwell to bring it to you."

"But I *have* my lunch money!"

"That's tomorrow's. You need today's."

I caught her meaning.

"While you make the call, I will talk to Mrs. Kalley and Betty will take care of anyone else who might be sitting around with overgrown ears. Come on."

We sauntered down the hall to the office. Mrs. Kalley was eating a sandwich at her desk.

"Well, Reubella, I've seen you in the office more today than all of last year and this year put together! What can I do for you this time?"

I wondered if she knew what she had done for me last time.

"I forgot today's lunch money. Could I please call home and ask someone to bring it to me?"

"Couldn't you borrow some money?"

I looked down at my feet. "I don't like to do that, Mrs. Kalley."

She believed me, as well she should. I *don't* like to be in debt.

"All right," she said. "Here's the phone. You other girls can wait in the hall until Reubella gets through calling."

I thought we were done for then, but reckoned without Debbie's inventiveness. "O.K.," she said amiably, and then, as though she had just noticed it, she said, "Gee, that's a pretty necklace you have on! I never saw one like it before."

"Oh, it sure is," Betty chimed in. Mrs. Kalley held it up for them to see and explained that it had been made for her by someone, but by that time I was dialing the number as hard as I could and hoping the girls could keep her occupied. I turned away from the desk so I could talk softly into the mouthpiece. Dad answered the phone.

"Hey, Dad—I have to speak to Ms. Cromwell quick!"

"What's wrong?"

"Can't explain," I hissed into the mouthpiece, "but there's been a foul-up about the team. We need her to straighten things out."

"Can I help?"

I was getting panicky. "No! It has to be Ms. Cromwell."

"She's out running—probably won't be back for half an hour."

I stifled a groan. "Well, tell her to come over soon as she gets home. And to come to the office and ask for me. Oh—and you might tell her she's bringing me some lunch money. And thanks!"

I hung up before he could say "but I gave you lunch money this morning." Mrs. Kalley had missed my whole conversation. I smiled nicely and thanked her for the use of the telephone. Then we went out.

"She wasn't there," I said as soon as we were out of earshot. "Dad's going to give her the message."

"Well, she'll get here," Debbie said confidently. "She'll tell old Prima where to get off."

"I hope so." But I wasn't sure that would be Ms. Cromwell's way of handling things.

The cafeteria is a noisy place. We're all required to eat there, whether we buy our lunch or bring it. I bought a sandwich and a salad, and the three of us sat down to eat. Soon Mrs. Kalley's voice came loudly over the intercom.

"Reubella Foster, would you please come to the office and get your lunch money."

I had a mouth full of sandwich.

"Quick! Shove the rest over here." Betty's long arm

swept the food toward her. I got up chewing and started out.

"Hey, Reubella—how many lunches do you *eat* a day?" some male voice hollered as I passed a table. "You want to hit six feet?"

I would've stuck out my tongue, but I hadn't swallowed all of my food yet.

Ms. Cromwell filled up the office with her powerful presence. She seemed to be holding herself in, even so.

"Thanks for coming over," I said. "You brought my lunch money?"

"It's in my shoulder bag." She said it a little louder than necessary, for Mrs. Kalley's benefit. We stepped out into the hall.

"That woman is inordinately curious!" she whispered with some vehemence. "I practically had to show her my social security number!"

"I can imagine," I said. "Look, Ms. Cromwell, we're in some kind of stupid mess over the basketball stuff." I explained as best I could what had transpired between Mr. Prima and me that morning and watched her face grow darker and more thunderous.

"That's incredible!" she burst out. "What an illogical, unreasonable decision! It makes no sense at all."

"We think so, too. Why don't you go talk to him? When he sees what a great person you are, he'll go to the School Board and get you authorized in no time. We girls could come along and back you up—"

Ms. Cromwell shook her head. "Probably that would be unwise. I shouldn't want you girls to be identified with me in the event I have to be obnoxious."

"Well, we aren't going to have a team anyway unless you win," I reasoned. "I don't mind being identified with you."

Just then the bell rang. "Run along to class," she told me. "I've no idea how things will turn out. But regardless of whether I change Mr. Prima's mind, get word to the girls to meet me after school at the drugstore. If we can't work out, we can at least get a milk shake."

I had every confidence that Ms. Cromwell would prevail, and would do so in such a way that Mr. Prima would not even know she had won. She, however, had a worried look when she waved me good-by.

After-lunch classes are hard enough to pay attention in even under the best of circumstances. That particular day, all of us who were on the team were fit to be tied, wondering how Ms. Cromwell had fared with Mr. Prima, or how we would ever be able to find out. I kept hoping for an announcement over the intercom that would say something terse and telling like: "The girls basketball team will practice on the playground this afternoon at three-oh-five."

The announcement never came. Within four minutes after the last bell, all of us converged on the sidewalk in front of the school. No one had heard anything.

"All right," I said. "To Bagley's drugstore. Forward march."

"Reubella! Reubella Foster! Would you wait just a moment, please!"

Without even turning around, I recognized Mr. Prima's voice.

"Uh-oh," said Betty. "He's coming this way, and he looks strange!"

"O.K. Break up and go to the drugstore in little bunches," I said under my breath. "I'll be there as soon as I can."

"But we can't leave you—"

"Quick!" I said. "Get out of here!"

Maybe it was because my eyes were bugging or something. They didn't argue anymore, but moved off in a hurry. I turned back to meet my fate.

"Yes, sir?"

He certainly was frowning, and his hair looked mussed.

"I'd like to see you in my office."

"All right." My heart was beating harder than usual. I hoped he couldn't see the pulse jumping in my throat. I certainly didn't want him to think I was upset or anything. I followed him along the gravel driveway and into the school.

"Now," he said, when we were in his office and I was again enthroned in the uncomfortable chair opposite his desk. "I feel that I was perfectly fair and reasonable with you this morning, Reubella."

I didn't say anything, just looked at him and waited for what he would say next.

"I explained to you *carefully* why there would be no girls basketball team this year."

I sat there.

"Your obstinacy in this matter has surprised me more than I can say—you always impressed me as a sensible, mature girl who wouldn't get mixed up in fruitless controversies."

At that point I experienced a tightness of the chest that comes of keeping the mouth shut when you want to argue. The problem was, I didn't know *how* I should argue, not knowing what Ms. Cromwell had said to him.

"What's the matter?" I asked. It was an innocent enough question. I didn't expect the reaction that followed.

"What's the matter! I'll tell you what's the matter. Your meddling friend Ms. Cromwell has threatened to report our school to the Department of Health, Education, and Welfare!" He sat back and glared at me as though I were personally responsible.

"But why would she do that?"

"A good question. Why indeed? She has no case at all." He slapped the arm of his chair for emphasis.

I felt I was slogging through a dense forest blind-folded. Ms. Cromwell had told him something that had him plenty worried. "Mr. Prima, I don't understand what you're talking about. You'll have to explain it to me."

"You needn't pretend innocence, young lady! I know you planned it together." He glared over the top of his glasses. "I certainly would have expected better of you."

I went back to the original question. "What happens if she reports our school?"

"They'll send people to investigate, of course, to find out if it's true."

"If *what* is true?"

"That we're violating Title IX guidelines."

I sighed. It felt to me as though we were speaking two different languages that had only a dozen words in common. I wondered why he had called me to his office. Did he intend to keep me there as hostage until Ms. Cromwell relented? Was he going to pick my brain to see how much I knew? Did I need a lawyer? It seemed wise not to volunteer any information or to do any explaining or arguing. *I* didn't know what "title nine" was—for all I knew it was *Gone with the Wind*—but he would never believe that, considering the mood he was in.

I suppose he came to the conclusion that my being there wasn't going to accomplish anything, because he said abruptly: "You're excused."

"Thank you." I got up and started out of his office in a daze.

"And, Reubella—"

"Yes, sir?"

"If, as a result of all this, our school's entire athletic program is crippled, I hope it will be a lesson to you never to act hastily to satisfy some selfish wish."

"Yes, sir." I didn't have the foggiest notion what he meant. I just wanted to get out of there.

It didn't surprise me that the Buxty Hooda was waiting, engine idling, when I came out the front door. I got in without a word, and Ms. Cromwell—her jaw set and nostrils flaring—drove away from the school. I hoped she wasn't mad at me, but I didn't have the energy to talk or ask questions. Part of me believed I was having a long nightmare and would wake up from it soon.

"Did he threaten you?" she asked, when we were almost to Bagley's.

"No, ma'am."

"It was cowardly of him to detain you. Order of peck, that's what!"

"What?"

"Order of peck. Hens in a chicken yard establish an order of peck. The top chicken can peck all the others and not be pecked by any. The second chicken can peck all the others except the top chicken, and so on down, until finally one poor fowl is pecked by them all and not allowed to peck any of the others. Your Mr. Prima behaves like the next-to-last chicken."

It was all too complicated for me. I stared glumly through the huge windshield and wondered how fortune could make a complete turnabout so quickly.

"No," said Ms. Smithers. "On the contrary, you know you dote on conflict."

"Am I that bad, really?"

"Yes. But it's all right, since you're usually right and you usually win."

I could hear Ms. Cromwell's boot heels thudding upon the porch as she paced. I felt a little guilty for eavesdropping, but not guilty enough to quit.

"It may not be all right this time," she said. "The girls stand to lose if I stir up trouble, and I don't want that to happen. But our cause is right. The community *must* make the same investment in its girls as it does in its boys. Heavens! You should see Betty—she's like a Zulu princess and is a splendid player. She should be on a college team next year, but how will they find her if she doesn't play?"

"Why are you so troubled about the hearing tomorrow night?" Ms. Nesselrode probed. "It seems to me that you have an open-and-shut case. All you are asking is that you be allowed to coach the girls and to use the goals on the school grounds after school hours. Why should you worry about losing?"

"Ah, yes—but, Holly, the truth is, that Mr. Prima causes me to lose patience. He is like a marshmallow. Frankly, I am afraid I am going to blow my top in a most unseemly way!"

"I see. Well, Ernestine and I would be happy to go along, if you feel that our being there would have a settling influence upon you."

"Yes, indeed!" Ms. Smithers was enthusiastic. "I could wear my red satin."

"You might rehearse your arguments with us," Ms. Nesselrode went on. "Then if at some point you feel it is better for you to be silent, one or both of us could take over, depending upon the mood of the School Board."

I stepped up on the porch as quietly as possible and let myself into the lobby.

And met with an unexpected sight. Dad was sitting at the desk, which by contrast with former times was piled high with papers. He looked worried and tired. His hair stood up in little tufts and his shirt was rumpled.

"Wow! You must've had a busy day," I said.

"That's the understatement of the year," Dad said grimly. "Hellish is a more accurate word."

"What's wrong?" I walked to the desk and peered over his shoulder. All I could see was a jumble of papers —some of them letters, others columns of figures or memoranda.

"What's wrong is that your dear old ladies keep adding names to the list of people they want to invite to their dedication ceremony. And they keep changing their minds about what they want to serve and about a hundred other things. They *say* they will leave the arrangements to me, but then they spring these surprises—"

"Then you will just have to take charge," I said. "Tell them no more changes. Tell them what is, is."

"You tell them!" He rose suddenly from the chair. Some of the papers flew up and floated slowly to the floor. "They don't *hear!* They don't *listen!* They're so wrapped up in their projects and plans that the real world doesn't mean anything to them."

I stood there with my mouth open. Could that be my own dreaming dad saying those words?

"And why are you staring at me that way?" he asked.

I closed my mouth. "No reason. Just getting my breath, that's all."

Dad wilted into the chair again, shaking his head. "I was a fool . . . a fool to take this job. There isn't enough money in the world to make it worth this daily hassle!"

That did not sound good to me. I put my hand on his shoulder to let him know we were in it together. "You were not a fool," I said. "No one could do better at this than you."

"Sure—I'd do fine if I didn't spend each day trying to make sense of something one of them has started. It's not going to be an Old Focus Home—it's going to be an Old Circus Home!"

That made me laugh, and after a couple of seconds he laughed too. He patted my hand that was resting on his shoulder. "Reubella, what would I do if you weren't here?"

"You might have to hire some help, once you noticed I was gone," I said. "But you would manage."

Dad looked back at the pile of papers on his desk and sighed. "Well, before this crowd of people descends, we'll have to hire extra help—no doubt about it."

"Is it going to be bad?"

"It would be manageable if we could freeze the plans right now—no more changes allowed."

I moved over and sat on the edge of the desk. "Can't you put your foot down?"

"Of course—but it's like putting my foot down in quicksand. Maybe Ms. Cromwell could persuade the other two. She's a shade more decisive than they."

"I don't know whether you should count on that—at least not until she straightens out the trouble between our team and the School Board."

"The what?" Dad looked alarmed. I hastened to explain what had happened in school that day. I told him about Title IX and what happened when schools got caught not complying.

"Ms. Cromwell has called for a meeting of the School Board tomorrow night," I said. "If things work out, maybe she can persuade them that she has the good of the community at heart. She doesn't want to make trouble—she just wants a girls team that'll beat the socks off every other team in the county."

Dad seemed to have forgotten his personal conflict with the ladies for the moment. "Mr. Prima is a smooth politician," he said. "One reason he has survived so long as principal is by being always on the right side of any conflict. He can probably make Ms. Cromwell look foolish."

"Yes, she knows that. That's why we need to be at the hearing tomorrow night."

"We?"

"The team—and as many parents as possible. You're the only one I've got."

"Huh-uh. Not me." Dad sat back, shaking his head. "I don't want anything to do with it. Ms. Cromwell got herself into this, she can get herself out. I have enough troubles without getting mixed up in some silly controversy."

"It's not a silly controversy! We won't have a team if Ms. Cromwell doesn't win her case. I won't get to play basketball and neither will a bunch of other girls." I jumped off the desk and faced him. "You wouldn't have to say anything at the meeting—just be there to show your support for Ms. Cromwell and us."

"I'm not sure I *do* support her. She's an old lady. How do I know she's any good as a coach?"

"You could come to our workouts and see for yourself —if we have any more. Trouble is, we can't do any kind of practices until the School Board authorizes her—Mr. Prima saw to that."

Dad fiddled with a pen lying on the desk, which meant he was thinking about it.

"Look—I'll make a bargain with you," I said, leaning over the desk until we were practically forehead to forehead. "If you will go to the hearing tomorrow night, I'll see to it that the ladies don't change plans on you anymore before the dedication ceremony."

"Are there questions which the Board would like to direct to Ms. Cromwell?" Mr. Partin asked.

"Am I to understand," said Mr. Belweather, "that you actually have three master's degrees as well as an honorary doctorate?"

"That is correct—in Science, in Drama, and in Physical Education."

The room buzzed. Dad grinned in spite of himself. There were no more questions from the Board. Mr. Partin invited questions from the audience.

A man stood up. "I don't especially have one for *her,* but I would like to ask the Board something. When Mr. Greenlief said he wasn't gonna coach the girls, did you all take back the extra money you give him to do it?"

The man sat down. People looked at each other and nodded. The room filled with murmurs. Mr. Partin tapped lightly on the table. "Would you like to answer that, Mr. Prima?"

Mr. Prima cleared his throat. "Well . . . ah . . . only one paycheck has gone out to the teachers since the Board made its decision. And of course you realize that I am not authorized to make changes in salaries."

"He sure does throw that word 'authorize' around," I said to Dad.

The man stood up again. "Well, are you gonna take it back?"

Mr. Prima shot a glance at Coach Greenlief, who was scowling intently. "The Board has to make that decision," he said.

Mr. Partin was cool. "What is the Board's pleasure?"

There was a brief silence, then Mrs. Dipple raised her hand. "I move that the portion of salary designated as compensation for coaching a girls team be taken out of Mr. Greenlief's check."

"Second," said Mrs. Selma.

"Is there any discussion?"

No one on the Board said anything, although some in the audience looked as though they would like to speak. The muscles along Mr. Greenlief's jawline twitched like snakes in a sack.

"All in favor of the motion?"

Six arms went up. Mr. Partin banged once with his mallet-gavel. "Motion carries. Mr. Prima, please see that the necessary changes are made in Mr. Greenlief's next paycheck."

"I don't suppose I have any say in this, huh?" Mr. Greenlief said suddenly, loudly.

"Would you like to be recognized, Mr. Greenlief?"

"I just want to put in my two cents worth, now that you've voted. I feel like with all the work I've put in since I've been coaching here, I ought to have some say-so about all this. It just might be time for y'all to start looking for another coach."

This made a lot of people uneasy, because Coach Greenlief had had two championship seasons in basketball, and folks hoped for a third.

"The Board has only taken back that part of your salary which was to compensate you for time spent with the girls team, Mr. Greenlief."

"Well, can I help it if I don't have time to do everything?"

It was an illogical question, but it threw everything into a state of confusion. Dad leaned over and whispered in my ear. "He's going to get them so twisted up they won't know what they voted on. They'll forget why we came tonight if someone doesn't get them back on the track."

Before I knew what he was doing, he was on his feet with his hand up in the air. Mr. Partin recognized him.

"Mr. Chairman," Dad said in his best actor voice, "I would like to remind the Board that it is meeting tonight to consider whether Ms. Constance Cromwell should be authorized to coach our girls basketball team. Would it be possible to redirect any statements or questions to that end?"

He sat down and I reached over and squeezed his hand. Mr. Partin thanked him, then called for questions or discussion. A number of parents spoke in Ms. Cromwell's favor. No one objected to her as coach. I began to relax, happy that there had been no bloodshed or name-calling. Just about the time Mr. Partin was ready to ask for a vote of authorization from the Board, Coach Greenlief raised his hand.

"Mr. Chairman, may I say something?"

"Yes, if it's relevant to this discussion."

"It's relevant, all right! I can't for the life of me see why nobody has brought it up before now. Has anyone bothered to ask how old this lady is?"

There was a horrified gasp all around, especially from the women present. Mr. Partin turned pink.

"There *is* a mandatory retirement age for school employees, you know." Mr. Greenlief did not try to hide his derision.

Mr. Partin turned helplessly to Ms. Cromwell, who arose once more to address the gathering.

"I am seventy-two years of age," she announced. "However, I think my age is not relevant in this case. The mandatory retirement age is for school employees. I would not be an employee, but a volunteer. What is relevant is my physical condition, which is excellent."

She turned and gave Coach Greenlief one of her piercing looks. "If there is any doubt in your minds about it, I will challenge Coach Greenlief to a five-mile foot race to be held whenever and wherever he chooses. I believe I can beat him both in time and endurance."

This time Mr. Partin's gavel could not still the commotion in the cafeteria. The hubbub continued for several minutes. The Board members consulted in whispers while the audience contemplated the excitement of a five-mile race between an old lady and the coach. Some people sitting next to Dad and me had already started making bets by the time Mr. Partin managed to reestablish order. Mr. Prima looked as though he had been through a wringer.

"Ladies and gentlemen," said Mr. Partin, "the School Board has no business except to decide on the question at hand, which is whether to authorize Ms. Cromwell as official coach of the girls team. We are ready to vote. Do I hear a motion that we so authorize Ms. Cromwell, and that she be allowed to work with the girls on the school grounds after school hours?"

"I so move!" the Reverend Mr. Hawkes shouted.

"Second!" echoed Mrs. Dipple.

"Discussion? All in favor of the motion!"

All hands went up. "Motion carried!" He banged the gavel hard on the table. "As there is no other business, this meeting of the School Board is adjourned."

A loud roar went up from the crowd, accompanied by clapping, stomping, and congratulations for Ms. Cromwell. Ms. Smithers and Ms. Nesselrode looked proud enough to explode.

It was quite late when the five of us finally made it through the throngs of people back to the Buxty Hooda.

"But what about Title IX?" I asked as we drove home. "Aren't you going to sick the Government on Mr. Prima?"

"No need for that," Ms. Cromwell said. "Once the team shows its stuff, threats won't be necessary. It's much better to have community support freely given than grudgingly yanked out piece by piece. By next year this time I can virtually promise that there will be as much money allocated for the girls as for the boys. As a matter of fact, we might think about building a new gym."

Dad, sitting next to me, sighed noisily as though to say Here we go again!

"Stephen, I want to thank you from the bottom of my heart," said Ms. Cromwell, turning in the driver's seat to look back at him. Ms. Smithers grabbed the wheel to keep the Buxty Hooda from running up on the curb. My ears perked up—it was the first time I could remember any of the ladies calling Dad by his first name.

"I don't understand," he said.

"Thank you for getting the meeting back on the track so skillfully tonight. You saved the day—or night, as it were."

Dad looked uncomfortable. I think it had only just dawned on him that he had stuck his neck out despite his best intentions.

"I'm making you a promise on behalf of all three of us," she went on. "You are from henceforth in charge of the dedication ceremony—all aspects of it. No meddling from us—absolutely!"

"Why—thank you. That will be helpful." He seemed stunned.

"Furthermore, we want you to know that we have great confidence in you as manager of the Home. We intend to be more cooperative and less self-centered. Feel free to develop and carry out your own ideas about how the Home shall be run."

We were pulling into the driveway by that time and I saw Dad's face under the streetlight. It was a strange mixture of astonishment, hope, and, above all, determination.

Ms. Cromwell gave us girls a talking to the day after the School Board hearing. She said it was absolutely imperative—those were her words—that we be humble, cooperative, industrious, and, most of all, silent. Not that we should never speak again, but we should not say smug things about our victory.

"Let your behavior be exemplary," she said. "This season you have a team, a schedule, and a bunch of 1932 gym suits. Next year you will have everything you deserve, including a place to practice. Your mothers and fathers will see to it."

So our workouts continued, rain or shine, on the Shad school grounds. People began dropping by to watch. The story of our three ladies was in the county newsweekly, including veiled references to the hearing, so scarcely an afternoon passed that did not see a small crowd gathered around our makeshift court, watching Ms. Cromwell put us through our paces. The attention made us self-conscious at first, but as we got into what we were doing, we forgot anyone was around. Soon we were playing like a well-oiled machine.

One day about halfway through our practice, the entire Varsity team, which includes Debbie's brother Steve, came jogging toward us across the field from the gym. My first thought was that Coach Greenlief, having heard that part of our training involved daily running, had decided his team should try it too. I expected they would jog by, favoring us with a few choice words as they passed.

But they didn't run by. Instead, they joined the group who had come to watch us. The coach wasn't with them. It was all very puzzling and took our minds off the game. We started missing easy shots and falling over our own feet.

Ms. Cromwell blew her silver whistle and called us over to the side, scanning our faces with her sharp eyes.

"I don't know why they are here either," she said to our unspoken question. "But one thing is certain—if you let their presence affect your playing that much, then you might as well quit now. You'll be no kind of team. You'll lose every game you play. Winning requires concentration and discipline—that's the only way you can be better than you are!"

Out of the corner of my eye I saw the boys grinning and poking at each other and making remarks. It made me furious! Ms. Cromwell was right—we should be so good that we could play even if a pack of chimpanzees came to watch.

It made a difference in our performance. As we ended our workout the small crowd applauded, including some of the boys. The gleam in Ms. Cromwell's eye said she was pleased with us.

Before I realized what she was up to, she strode over to Debbie's brother and said, "You're Steve Claymore, aren't you?"

"Yes, ma'am." He took a step backward.

"I'm Constance Cromwell." She put out her hand and Steve was forced to take it, although you could tell he wasn't used to shaking old ladies' hands. The other boys edged away, but he couldn't follow as long as she had his hand in her firm grip. "Would you introduce me to your teammates?"

No one ignores Ms. Cromwell's requests. Besides, Steve was relieved to have an excuse to call them back, not wanting to be left alone. "Yes, ma'am—sure! Hey, you guys come here—Ms. Cromwell wants to meet you."

They came back reluctantly. This time *they* were falling over their feet. Steve introduced them all, and as Ms. Cromwell shook the hand of each one, she looked him in the eye as though memorizing his life and times. It took the starch out of them.

"Now," she said, when she had shaken the last hand, "I want to know why you are not practicing in the gymnasium this afternoon even though you are dressed out."

A person does not tell Ms. Cromwell "It's none of your business." Steve and the others looked at each other.

"We just wanted to see y'all play," he said finally.

"And where is Coach Greenlief?"

"He . . . has a strained leg muscle."

"Yeah," said Rob Tompkins. "He hurt it running."

"Running?" Ms. Cromwell's eyebrows climbed. "Coach Greenlief is running?"

"Yes, ma'am. Or at least he was until he hurt his leg. We found out when we got to the gym this afternoon."

"I see. So since you had no supervision you decided to come out here." She seemed satisfied with their explanation. "All right—now that you've seen them play, what do you think?"

"What do we think? Y-you mean, of the girls?" Steve stammered.

"No. Of their teamwork." Ms. Cromwell suppressed a smile.

"They're good," Rob said. "As a team, they're better than we are—work together better than we do, I mean."

The others looked at him as though he had uttered blasphemy. As for us girls, we couldn't believe our ears.

"Thank you," said Ms. Cromwell, giving Rob a special smile. "And now—it's been a rugged afternoon. Reubella, I believe we should invite everyone over to the Home for lemonade and cookies. What do you think?"

"Wh-why, yes—sure! It's a great idea, only—"

She didn't wait to hear my "only," because everyone was yelling and cheering. "You, too," she told the boys. "As soon as you get dressed, come over. Girls! Into the van! You can shower and dress at the Home."

I was uneasy. When she started the engine and got the Buxty Hooda underway, I said I didn't think Dad would have provisions at the Home for such a large group.

"Oh, I'm sure that's true. I have an emergency supply back there, though." She motioned toward the rear of the van where the other girls were chattering and screeching. I wondered what she had, short of five loaves and two fishes, that would feed thirty-odd thirsty, hungry teen-agers. I also envisioned Dad's reaction when the girls scattered throughout the house to use the showers and leave the bathrooms all asteam. He had taken new heart since Ms. Cromwell, Ms. Nesselrode, and Ms. Smithers had given their promise to let him manage the Home without interference. He had hired a part-time cook, a secretary, and a cleaning crew. He also engaged Mirelda Matthews to serve as tour guide when visitors came to look over the place. There had been lots of visitors of late, as word of the three ladies and the Old Focus Home spread. I wasn't sure but what he would consider this invasion by the team an instance of Ms. Cromwell's going back on her word. But before I could mention my worries, she changed the subject.

"Why do you suppose Coach Greenlief is running, Reubella?"

"I don't know—getting in shape, I guess. Coaches have to be in shape to keep up with the players. *You* know that—look how many miles you run every day."

"Yes—but I have a feeling that Mr. Greenlief is on the verge of accepting my challenge to a race. That is, if the muscle he has strained isn't too seriously hurt."

I stared. "Do you think he will?"

"His pride suffered an enormous blow the night of the hearing. So yes—I think he is about ready."

"But how can he get ready in a couple of weeks? Gosh, you've been running for years!"

"Yes," she said, sighing, "and therein lies the problem. I am not a young woman anymore, Reubella."

"You can beat him," I said.

"Perhaps." She didn't seem to want to talk about it anymore. I settled into silence and thought about how Dad was going to look when the van disgorged this crowd on the porch of the Old Focus Home.

The noise and chatter brought him flying to the front door looking a bit pale. His lips formed the beginning of a question which Ms. Cromwell gave him no time to ask.

"Stephen, these girls are perishing of thirst and hunger. Furthermore, they are about to be joined by a contingent of young men suffering from the same ailment. We need quantities of cookies and lemonade."

"But, Ms. Cromwell, we don't have—"

"Yes, we do. Just a moment." She went to rummage in the back of the van. She returned shortly with three cans of powdered lemonade and eight boxes of cookies. "Just find me a large container, about the size of a dye vat. Ernestine and Holly and I will do the mixing. Reubella, the young ladies need to shower and dress—show them to the bathrooms."

"But . . . but Ms. Cromwell," Dad tried again. "I'm afraid this isn't a good time—"

"Don't worry, Stephen," she said, patting his shoulder. "Holly and Ernestine and I will take care of this. You just enjoy yourself, meeting the young people."

I didn't have time to hang around to see how Dad took it. First I went to fetch Ms. Nesselrode and Ms. Smithers from the pursuit of their respective arts. Then I showed the girls where to shower and dress. In no time at all my friends, who had never before been inside our house, were all over the place. They oohed and ahhed and admired everything, from the statue of Robert E. Lee which now stood in the lobby, to the rock and shell collection in Ms. Cromwell's special room. Ms. Nesselrode agreeably turned her stereo to the radio station most patronized by the teen-age population of Shad, and soon the house was filled with unaccustomed sound.

When the boys finally arrived, the lemonade had been mixed and Ms. Smithers was furiously ladling it into paper cups. Ms. Nesselrode was in charge of seeing that the trays were heaped with cookies. Ms. Smithers smiled so much her eyes almost disappeared.

"I just love a party, don't you?" she said to me. "Especially when the joint is jumping!" She did a few quick dance steps behind the serving table and kicked her heels together.

"Yes, ma'am," I said, "but I sure never expected to see anything like this in the Old Focus Home."

"Whyever not? Always expect the unexpected—it's what makes life exciting, right up to the last moment, Reubella."

She sounded a bit severe about it. I took one of the trays of cookies and began to circulate with it through the house, noting that someone had put a paper cup in the outstretched hand of the statue of Robert E. Lee. In the music room a person was playing pop tunes on Ms. Nesselrode's Steinway. Several couples danced in the downstairs hallway. Noise and laughter came from every corner. I loved it!

I started upstairs to look for Dad, who seemed to have disappeared sometime during the first few minutes of the invasion. Just as I reached the landing, the doorbell rang. The sound startled me, because people hardly ever use the doorbell. Either they knock, or they walk right in. Puzzled, I set the tray on the landing and went down to open the door.

Six people I had never laid eyes on in my life stood on our porch—three men and three women. They looked very efficient and businesslike.

"Good afternoon," said the short bald man nearest the doorbell. "I am Dr. Edward Nickerson from the Duke University Center for the Study of Aging and Human Development. Is this the Old Focus Home of Shad?"

"Yes, sir." The noises of the party drifted over my shoulder and out into the open air.

"I . . . uh . . . was in touch with a Mr. Foster, who I believe manages the Home?"

"Yes, sir, that's right."

"He suggested that we bring a delegation down today to tour the facility and to interview the residents."

The party noises seemed louder than ever, and his face registered doubt. As for me, I finally knew the meaning of the word "dismayed."

"Well, I'm Reubella, Mr. Foster's daughter. Won't you come in?" I stood aside, and they filed in. I could certainly understand their astonishment. The joint was jumping, all right. The statue of Robert E. Lee stared blankly at them and held out its paper cup. "I was just looking for Dad when the doorbell rang. If you would sit here in the lobby—"

Most of the chairs were occupied by my friends, but I shooed them away and saw that the delegation was settled, then sped off to find Ms. Cromwell. She was in the rock room giving three of the guys some pointers on purchasing scuba diving equipment. I told her about the delegation from the Center for Aging. Her hand went to her throat.

"So that's why Stephen was so upset! I didn't understand—oh, dear!"

"Where is he, Ms. Cromwell? Those people out there seem nervous."

She excused herself and swept from the room. The guys and I followed as she showered orders left and right. "Reubella, don't go looking for your father just yet. Boys, you must round up your teammates and depart. The party has been shortened due to circumstances beyond our control. Holly! Ernestine! Come quickly!"

Ms. Cromwell's major-general voice is handy in such emergencies. Soon everyone except Dad had converged in the lobby. It was a crowded place. Ms. Nesselrode and Ms. Smithers introduced themselves to the puzzled delegation and kept them occupied while Ms. Cromwell and I said good-by to my friends and saw them out. When the door shut behind the last one, there was a great, shuddering silence. I felt as though I had suddenly gone deaf.

"Get your father, Reubella," she said in a low voice. "The day of reckoning is upon us."

I wanted to remind her that it hadn't been my idea, but I didn't.

When I am in a snit, I always try to get as close to the river as I can, not because I intend to jump in and end it all, but because the river can make me feel peaceful again. I wasn't sure whether Dad felt that way, but I went outside nevertheless, hoping he might be there. The sun had gone down, but there was still light enough for me to make out his figure on the pier silhouetted against the evening sky.

I called him as I crossed the yard. He didn't budge. He may as well have been the statue of Robert E. Lee. I walked out to the end of the pier where he stood looking at the river.

"Dad?" I tugged his jacket sleeve. "Didn't you hear me call you? Some people from Duke are here to see you."

"I'm not here." His voice was cold.

"The man—Dr. Nickerson—said you had invited them."

"That was when I thought there was something here worth seeing." His voice rose and so did his temper. "You and your Ms. Cromwell blew it!"

"Dad, I'm sorry. I tried to tell her you needed advance notice, but—"

"Too bad she didn't listen. But what can you expect?"

It was certainly no time for me to try to justify Ms. Cromwell's actions, even though I felt Dad was taking it too hard. After all, the Old Focus Home was the ladies' home now. They should have some say-so about inviting friends over. I sympathized and reasoned, hoping to persuade him that he'd better get in the house and meet the delegation, otherwise Ms. Cromwell, Ms. Nesselrode, and Ms. Smithers might unwittingly make things worse. He just looked at the river, stony-faced and angry.

"What does the house look like right now?" he asked suddenly.

I had a vision of paper cups scattered about, cookie crumbs, disarranged furniture, and although I hadn't checked out the bathrooms since the girls used the showers, I was fairly sure they were far from spotless.

"It's in sort of a mess," I said in a small voice. "But it won't take any time to straighten things up. I'll do it myself, right after dinner."

"Ah, yes. Dinner. Hazel Jackson was supposed to cook and serve dinner. But when you and your horde descended, she threw up her hands and left. She said no civilized person should be expected to work in any such uproar. But I don't suppose you knew that."

I shook my head dumbly. Things were even worse than I had thought. It was dark now, and the chill had gotten through my sweater to my bones. I began to shiver.

"Oh, to hell with it!" he said, kicking a loose plank. "Come on—I may as well make the best of a bad situation. But it's so humiliating!"

We went up the back steps to the kitchen. Delicious smells greeted us the minute Dad opened the door. Ms. Smithers, attired in caftan and borrowed apron, was busy at the stove, humming and dancing as she worked. Every burner had a bubbling saucepan. A large bowl of salad sat ready upon the counter.

"Well, Stephen—thank goodness! I was so worried!" She danced over and kissed his cheek. In his dumb-founded state he could do nothing but take it. "Dinner will be ready in about fifteen minutes. Do go in and meet Dr. Nickerson and his friends—they're perfectly delightful."

She pushed him gently toward the dining room, where Ms. Nesselrode was setting the large table. She, too, was relieved to see Dad, and kissed him on the other cheek. I wondered if they feared he had hurled himself into the river.

"Constance has been frantic with worry, Stephen. *Please* go assure her that you're all right—she's in the music room with the visitors."

Dad didn't say anything, just looked around the dining room and then headed for the lobby. I followed. The furniture was in place. Not a crumb, not a paper cup was visible. The general's hand was empty once more.

"Swept under the rug," Dad muttered, but he certainly had no cause to complain about the appearance of things.

Even before we reached the music room we could

hear Ms. Cromwell's voice booming forth as she explained about Ms. Nesselrode's musical career and the Concertoratorio.

"Holly plans to perform the piano solo herself at the premiere," she was saying. Then she caught sight of Dad and me in the doorway and her face lighted up.

"Reubella, you found him! Oh, Stephen, thank goodness!" She swooped toward him and gave him a great hug that disconcerted him entirely.

"I wasn't lost," he said in a smothered voice.

"Dr. Nickerson, this is Stephen Foster, our Manager and Creative Thinker." She regarded Dad with tremendous pride. Dad shook hands with the doctor and the other members of the group.

"Mr. Foster, I must say, I've never seen anything like this in my life."

"I'm not surprised. I want to apologize for any inconvenience—"

"Please, don't! We've had a fine time talking to these ladies. You have a splendid facility here—so different from the usual institution for senior citizens."

There were nods all around. I took it this delegation had seen a lot of retirement homes. Ms. Cromwell glowed. Dad showed signs of relaxing some.

A short time later the eleven of us were seated around the large dining table gorging on Chinese food—that is, inasmuch as you can gorge if you aren't too good with chopsticks. Dr. Nickerson and his friends were full of questions. How had the ladies decided to start the Home? What sort of business arrangements had it involved? Why did they pick Shad? Having heard most of it before, and being more interested in the food, I did not pay a great deal of attention until Dr. Nickerson turned to Ms. Nesselrode and asked point blank who the other residents were.

"Well," she said, delicately maneuvering her chopsticks, "you see, there are no other residents . . . yet."

"But of course there will be?"

"Of course. We've only just gotten under way. We haven't even had the dedication ceremony."

"What sort of screening process do you intend to use, Mr. Foster?"

"Screening process?" Dad looked blank.

"How will you screen applicants?"

Dad put down his fork. None of the ladies had ever mentioned accepting applications. Nevertheless, his actor training stood him in good stead.

"We're working on that right now," he said, as though it were true. "Certainly, those who apply should be prepared to keep up the vigorous pace set by these three." He smiled around the table, but I wasn't fooled—his eyes weren't smiling. "You never know when a bunch of teen-agers is going to drop in unexpectedly for cookies and lemonade."

Dr. Nickerson chuckled. "Yes, indeed! For a few minutes this afternoon I thought we had come to the wrong place. One never sees that sort of thing, you know—a retirement home overrun with teen-agers!"

Ms. Cromwell spoke up. "One of the serious mistakes in the present concept of retirement homes is that people of the same age live in them. Older folks need involvement with people of all ages. Right now, I coach a high school basketball team and a women's track team. Holly teaches piano to half the town, and Ernestine is giving instruction in painting and sculpture to anyone who wants it, from age eight to eighty. It makes for a nice mixture wandering in and out."

"Well, then," said Dr. Nickerson, "I suppose that means that whoever applies for a place here has to want to stay involved with the rest of the world. Many older people don't want that at all—they look forward to peace and quiet."

Ms. Smithers snorted. "They only *think* that's what they want! Two weeks of it and they're bored silly. A person doesn't automatically shut down and withdraw at a certain age. One's whole life is a struggle for balance between being out there in the thick of things and withdrawing to a quiet place. It shouldn't be all work and then all rest. That's not normal."

"I know some people who would like to live here," said Dr. Nickerson. "Shall I encourage them to apply?"

The three ladies looked at each other. Ms. Smithers twisted her napkin round and round, and Ms. Cromwell cracked her knuckles.

"We're happy that you like what you've seen, Dr. Nickerson," Ms. Nesselrode said carefully. "However, we're not quite ready to open the Home to other applicants. If you'll leave your address, Stephen will get in touch with you later, I'm sure."

"I understand," said Dr. Nickerson, but he sounded puzzled.

After dinner I helped put away the food and clean up the kitchen while Dad and the delegation conferred in the lobby. The three ladies did not talk much as we passed each other back and forth between kitchen and dining room. They seemed preoccupied. The conversation at dinner had set me to thinking for the first time about the future of the Home. Would it just be our three ladies, or would it eventually be overrun with others of their kind? I wondered why they were so reluctant to talk about it.

The day ended on a peaceful note. Forgiveness was in the air. Dr. Nickerson seemed impressed with Dad's imagination and his projected plans for the Home, which naturally made Dad more expansive than ever. By the time our guests were settled in their rooms for the night, Dad had quite forgotten his afternoon anger. The last thing he said to me as he told me good night was to be sure to have my friends over again very soon.

Just before drifting off to sleep, I remembered Coach Greenlief's injured leg muscle and Ms. Cromwell's prediction that he was about to accept her challenge. Sometime during the night I dreamed that the two of them were competing in the Olympics before thousands of spectators, and I held the starting gun.

I do not believe that I am one of those people who can prophesy and predict things, but what happened next certainly did seem to be my dream coming true. Only a few days after the delegation from the Center for Aging had come and gone, Ms. Cromwell received a telephone call from Coach Greenlief while we were eating breakfast. He reminded her that she had challenged him to a five-mile race in the presence of practically the whole town. Then he offered a counterchallenge—fifteen miles on the quarter-mile track at school the very next Saturday at 10:00 A.M. The suddenness of it all took Ms. Cromwell's breath.

"Fifteen miles, Mr. Greenlief? Did you say *fifteen?*"

"You heard me right, Ms. Cromwell. What's the matter—too tough for you?"

"I should say not! I'm just amazed, that's all."

"Fifteen miles is a *real* race, Ms. Cromwell—a test of speed *and* endurance."

"You're certainly right about that, Mr. Greenlief. All right—I accept. Next Saturday at the school. Ten o'clock."

She banged the receiver down and, when she had calmed down enough to do so, reported the part of the coffee and stirred it with her knife. But the worst of it is, she drank the stuff and didn't even know the difference!"

"Well," I said, "it seems to me that the main thing she needs is the energy to endure for fifteen miles. I don't know how we can give her that."

Ms. Nesselrode sighed and sat down at her Steinway. For several minutes she played snatches of pieces, flitting from one melody to another in a distracted way. "We must put ourselves in her place. If *I* were about to do something so crucial as running a fifteen-mile race, what would help me most?"

"I don't know about you," I said, "but I would want a huge cheering section of my friends. I mean *real* friends —not the sort who would start cheering for the other side if it looked like I was about to lose."

Ms. Nesselrode's fingers did flip-ups on the keys and came down hard in a mush of notes. "Why, of course! How would we manage without your good sense? That's exactly what she needs!"

She leaped from the piano bench, unlocked the door, and disappeared down the hall. When I left for school next morning she was on the phone speaking very softly with her hand cupped around the mouthpiece. Ms. Smithers hovered, grinning, nearby.

That day I came home and shut myself up in my room to study for an algebra test, so I was not aware of what was going on under my very nose—or to be more accurate, under my feet. About five there came a light tap on my door.

"Come in!" I yelled.

Ms. Smithers' orange head poked around the door, her face ringed with merriment. "You must come down immediately, Reubella. Hurry!"

I jumped up from my desk and followed a trail of giggles along the dark hallway and down the stairs.

You will have a hard time believing what I saw below,

even after I tell you that I saw it—them—with my own eyes. The lobby appeared to be jammed, packed with people, but after my senses returned to normal I counted only six besides Ms. Nesselrode and Ms. Smithers. Ms. Cromwell was nowhere in sight.

"And this is Reubella, whose idea it was," Ms. Smithers said, taking my hand and pulling me toward the waiting group. It is probably a good thing, because my impulse was to turn around and run upstairs again.

"*She* said that a cheering section of loyal friends would do more for Connie than anything else—and here you are! Let me introduce you."

First was Mr. Willis, about my height with wide shoulders and crinkly blue eyes, a minister by profession. Next came Mr. Wilhelm the weight lifter, huge and muscular with a shock of thick, gray hair and hands the size of dinner plates. Ms. Staley, in gray fur coat and cloche hat, resembled a tragic Russian queen but actually ran a combination bookstore and delicatessen. Gentlemanly Mr. Hatchett, retired judge, was slightly stooped and made no bones about the fact that he adored Ms. Smithers. Ms. Taylor, black hair streaked with gray, had snapping black eyes and was President Emeritus of Moriah College. Dr. Kandy, although he looked like an elderly hippy with his leather breeches and green silk shirt, was actually a college professor. Ms. Smithers and Ms. Nesselrode filled me in on all the particulars as I tried very hard to be cool and not stare too much.

"Constance doesn't know they're here," Ms. Nesselrode said, beside herself with glee. "They've hidden their means of transport all up and down the street in other people's driveways. What a marvelous surprise!"

I thought fleetingly of Ms. Cromwell jogging grimly around the quarter-mile track at the school, ignorant of these goings-on. I hoped she wouldn't be *too* surprised.

"I guess Dad knows about this," I ventured.

133

"Of course he does—ever since this morning. Hazel has prepared a scrumptious dinner—"

At that moment heavy footsteps were heard on the porch and shortly the front door burst open. Ms. Cromwell, in sweat suit and track shoes, bounded into the lobby. "That rascal Greenlief—standing by the track the whole time I was running, putting me off my pace—"

Then her eyes grew accustomed to the indoor light, and she saw who was standing in the lobby. Her mouth opened. Her hands went up in the air.

And Ms. Cromwell fainted dead away.

The Old Focus Home was all excitement and noise during the next few minutes. Ms. Cromwell was descended upon, borne up, subjected to cold compresses, spirits of ammonia, and gentle slaps, all of this under a rain of concerned murmurs. When she finally opened her eyes she was settled on the couch with her head in the lap of Mr. Wilhelm the weight lifter, and her feet being rubbed by Ms. Staley.

"I didn't expect it to be like this," she said weakly.

"Expect what to be like what?" Mr. Willis asked.

"Dying and going to heaven. It was so sudden. I was going to race tomorrow, you know."

"And you still are," Ms. Nesselrode said with conviction. "You are very much alive, and so are we."

"But I never thought we'd all be together again in this life!" Ms. Cromwell looked about her at the faces, drinking them in. "How did you get here?"

"We dropped everything and took the fastest form of transportation from where we happened to be," Mr. Wilhelm said, looking at her with great tenderness. That in itself was a revelation, as I had never thought of Ms. Cromwell as a person to provoke tender feelings in anyone.

"We came to see the race," said Ms. Taylor, patting Ms. Cromwell's sturdy leg.

At the mention of the race Ms. Cromwell's expression clouded. "You came to see me lose. Coach Greenlief has it in the bag—he *must,* if he can waste time the very day before the race watching *me.*"

"He's just trying to psych you out," I said. "He can't beat you."

She sighed. "Reubella, I hate to let you and the team down—"

"You're not letting us down! I just wish we knew his strategy—all he's thinking of is revenge. He wants you to look ridiculous."

She sat up suddenly. "He can't trip me right out there in front of all the people. They'd ride him out of town on a rail!"

"Right. So he'll do something sneaky that'll make him look good and you look bad."

"It's so pointless. Nothing will be gained. I wish there were some way to prove to him that I don't want to be his arch enemy." She lay back in Mr. Wilhelm's lap. "There's nothing to do but go out and run as well as I can."

"And we will be beside the track urging you on," Professor Kandy said fervently. A chorus of cheers went up. Ms. Cromwell seemed somewhat comforted.

The Home glowed that evening, and for the first time I caught hold of a piece of the dream. At dinner I laughed so much my ribs ached and my face muscles twitched. Afterward we all sat before the fire. The older people reminisced and caught up on personal news. Dad and I were included as though we had always been a part of the strange and wonderful gathering.

I let myself think how it would be if these people came to live with us. We might have to add on to the house. We would become world famous. Dad would see the fruits of his labors, and I would not have to go far away to find a satisfying life. Ms. Smithers was right—adventure was everywhere, if you could only recognize it.

The next day could not have been more beautiful if it had been especially ordered. November, being new, had not yet gotten a good hold on things. The leaf colors were brilliant, the sky cloudless, and the air Indian Summer warm. As might be expected, the glow of the previous evening had paled some as anxiety about the race returned.

Still, everyone tried to be cheerful at breakfast. Hazel had fixed waffles and sausage, but the guests sort of picked at the food halfheartedly. Ms. Cromwell claimed that, as the runner, she couldn't eat a great deal without posing a threat to her chances of winning. The rest of us didn't have that excuse. Hazel passed in and out of the dining room, looking at the still-full plates and shaking her head. The general state of mind did not escape Ms. Cromwell, despite the bright chatter of her friends.

"All of you are taking this entirely too seriously!" she shouted suddenly, banging her fist upon the table and making the silverware leap. "If I win, I win. If I lose, I lose. That's the way of races. *I* don't mind losing—if I've run my best!"

Her words had a sobering effect. The chatter died away. "Yes," said Mr. Willis. "And we are with you all the way."

"Besides," Ms. Cromwell continued, "some good has already come of it, even if I lose. Coach Greenlief was overweight and paunchy, but this practicing to race has trimmed him down. He's gotten some muscle on him. I'm rather proud of him, to tell the truth. I shan't mind losing nearly so much to someone who has gone to such great trouble to beat me."

13

When we arrived at the school a half hour before the race was to begin, the town had already assembled and, from the looks of things, had been there since early morning. You would have thought it was the State Fair. A contingent of elderly people from the County Nursing Home in wheelchairs and folding chairs sat beside the track near the starting block. Over their heads flew a banner which read:

CONNIE CROMWELL—OUR WONDER WOMAN!
"Show 'em that Old ain't Dead, Connie!"

There was a concession stand and a souvenir booth. Bleachers had been brought out of the school gym and set up for the spectators. People milled about. Children scuffled in the dirt. The animal population was present in large numbers, mostly in the form of dogs and sparrows. Dad and I rode in the Buxty Hooda with our three ladies, while Mr. Willis followed next in his yellow VW. Ms. Staley roared behind him on a Honda motorcycle, Professor Kandy lumped along in an antique Packard, and Judge Hatchett and Ms. Taylor brought up the rear in a rented Checker cab. We were a circus parade and a convoy rolled into one. There was much cheering from the crowd as Ms. Cromwell descended from the Buxty Hooda in her 1932 gym suit and brand-new track shoes.

Mr. Willis, Professor Kandy, and Dad got folding chairs for all of us and set them up in a double row near the railing. Ms. Nesselrode and Ms. Smithers sat side by side under Ms. Nesselrode's big umbrella, both of them looking worried. I calculated that Ms. Cromwell and Coach Greenlief would have to circle the track sixty times in order to run fifteen miles. I wished the day were not quite so warm and that Ms. Cromwell were not so old.

I had a bad case of the fidgets and had to get up and walk around. Because the race had made the wire service, Shad was infested with curiosity seekers, including television and newspaper people. Cameras were set up all over the place, and the television crews wandered in and out among the spectators, interviewing anyone who knew anything about either of the runners. I saw a man with a microphone headed in my direction and I beat a hasty retreat, only to collide with another one coming from the opposite direction.

"Hello, young lady!" He had blond curly hair and a huge voice. He was three inches shorter than I, and much wider. The sun was in his eyes as he squinted up at me.

"Hello." I started to move on.

"I'm told that you're a friend of Constance Cromwell. Is that true?"

"I guess."

"Could you tell our TV audience your name?"

"Foster," I mumbled, looking away to some distant place. "If you'll excuse me—"

He was intent on his purposes. "Foster? That's an unusual name for a girl."

I wanted to say not nearly as unusual as my other name, but I didn't. He kept sticking the microphone in my face, making me cross-eyed.

"What do you think of Ms. Cromwell's chances, Foster?"

I gave him what I hoped was a stony look. "They are better than those of the average middle-aged overweight person," I said, looking hard at his paunchy front. I hoped the television audience would get the drift of my meaning.

The man clutched his microphone close to himself as though to hide the offending paunch and thanked me for my statement. He did not waste any more time on me, which suited me fine. It seemed safe at that point to go sit with Ms. Cromwell's cheering section.

The public-address system came on with a loud squeal, and from the platform by the track the announcer began.

"Ladies and gentlemen, may we have your attention please! The starting gun is due to go off in exactly five minutes. Please find a place behind the barricade. We must ask everyone to stay off the track for the duration of the race. Thank you."

"I wish," Ms. Smithers whispered, "that there were some legal way to obstruct Mr. Greenlief's progress."

"Bath oil wouldn't work on a dirt track," I said. "Besides, Ms. Cromwell would say it's unsportsmanlike. She wouldn't want to win on a fluke."

A roar went up from the crowd as Ms. Cromwell and Coach Greenlief walked out to the edge of the track and shook hands. The coach's nylon running suit bore the Shad school colors of purple and gold. Smiling and confident, he did little springing-up-and-down things, probably to show what good shape he was in. He waved at the crowd like he was Muhammad Ali or somebody. I thought he was a hot dog.

Not that Ms. Cromwell didn't look equally confident, but she seemed weighted down by being the crowd favorite. She didn't smile much, just lifted her hand once and ducked her head to acknowledge the cheers. Mr. Willis, Mr. Wilhelm, Judge Hatchett, Professor Kandy, Ms. Staley, and Ms. Taylor all stood and yelled and blew kisses. Ms. Nesselrode, Ms. Smithers, Dad, and I stayed put and kept our mouths shut. Frankly, I was worried, not so much that Ms. Cromwell couldn't endure, but that Coach Greenlief was up to something underhanded and there was nothing any of us could do.

The crowd became hushed as the two runners took their places at the starting block. The gun was raised, the starter's hand came down, the air was cut with a pistol shot, and they were off under a rain of cheers.

I could see in the first minute that Coach Greenlief was in good shape, sure enough. He was halfway around the track in a whiz. Mr. Wilhelm, standing behind me, clutched at the back of my chair and muttered words that I couldn't hear clearly. I caught snatches of things like ". . . can't possibly keep up that pace . . ." and ". . . is going to pull a muscle." I wished he would keep it to himself—Ms. Smithers and Ms. Nesselrode were nervous enough as it was.

Coach Greenlief did the four-lap mile in six and a half minutes according to Mr. Wilhelm's stopwatch. Mr. Wilhelm admitted that was excellent time. Ms. Cromwell lagged behind by a good thirty seconds. I watched her face, hoping she would wave at us when she passed, but her eyes were straight ahead. She was concentrating on the running and nothing else.

Coach Greenlief, on the other hand, was very conscious of his audience. He kept glancing sideways at the crowd. It was easy to tell which sections were for him and which were for Ms. Cromwell. Most of his applause came from the boys basketball team and from Mr. Prima. Hers was from the Senior Citizens' corner, the little knot of visiting friends, and the girls team. All in all, it was a pretty noisy place with all the yelling and whistling.

Gradually the spring began to go out of Coach Greenlief's step, even though he kept up the pace he had set from the beginning. At the end of the fifth mile Ms. Cromwell had gained on him some, but was still two minutes behind his time. The sun climbed higher—perspiration poured from their reddening faces. The coach's shaggy mustache, looking like a well-soaked paintbrush, sprayed droplets of sweat as he ran. The bloomer legs of Ms. Cromwell's 1932 gym suit sagged and flopped around her knees. Ms. Nesselrode pressed a nervous hand to her mouth, and Ms. Smithers shredded the Kleenex she was holding into a hundred bits. The cheering died down—the whole gathering took on a tense, forgetting-to-breathe feeling. I got up and moved to sit next to Dad. He reached over and squeezed my hand.

"I'm scared," I whispered in his ear. "Ms. Cromwell's face is too red."

He nodded. "I know. I'm a bit worried myself. We really should have kept her from doing this, even if it meant locking her in her room."

"I couldn't bear it if something happened to her—I think I would hate Coach Greenlief all the rest of my days!"

"Well," said Dad, looking around, "if he has any tricks, I wish he'd go ahead and pull them. At least the race would be over then, and Ms. Cromwell wouldn't have to run anymore."

But if Coach Greenlief had a plan that would rescue him, there was no evidence of it. He finished the seventh mile and began the eighth. His movements had become stiff and automatic. He picked up his feet and set them down, but the length of his stride got shorter and shorter. Ms. Cromwell ran steadily, smoothly.

"She's gaining!" Mr. Wilhelm shouted gleefully, slapping Mr. Willis on the back. "Got her second wind now—she's going to beat him!"

A surge of noise went up from the Senior Citizens. They waved their banner, yelling and cackling and cracking jokes about the coach.

Mr. Willis was more cautious. "Well, I hope nothing happens until she's up to his time—if the race stopped right now, he'd still be declared the winner."

Almost before the words were out of his mouth, Coach Greenlief stumbled and went down on one knee. Ms. Cromwell, a quarter of a track length behind him, saw it happen and her mouth opened in horror. Her pace slowed. Mr. Wilhelm was at the railing in a flash calling to her through cupped hands.

"Don't stop, Connie!" he bellowed. "Keep running— we'll take care of him!"

"But . . . he's hurt . . . ," she panted as she came our way.

Mr. Wilhelm's great dinner-plate hands gestured her on. "Don't you dare stop now!" he said fiercely. "Every Senior Citizen in Shad is counting on you!"

Ms. Cromwell's mouth snapped shut, she faced forward and continued her run. Meantime the coach had gotten up and started running again, but it wasn't exactly what you would call running anymore. He took a few more pitiful steps and then staggered to the side, putting a hand on the barricade to catch himself. He was shaking his head, as though he couldn't believe what was happening to him. I remembered what he had said to me that day in his office—*I am going to win because I am forty years younger and in better shape than Ms. Cromwell. Not to mention that she is female and naturally weaker.* It was clear to me now that my suspicions had been unfounded—he had really believed all those things!

Mr. Willis and Mr. Wilhelm were first to reach the exhausted challenger. They got on either side of him, draped his arms over their shoulders, and carted him off the track. What with all the sweat in his eyes and the pain of his cramped muscles, Coach Greenlief failed to see the irony of being borne up by two elderly men.

The turn of events created confusion—some thought the race should be stopped. Others wanted to see how long Ms. Cromwell could run. The spectators in the bleachers took it upon themselves to try to influence Ms. Cromwell.

"That's enough!" one section yelled.

"No! Keep going!" yelled another.

Mr. Wilhelm left the coach in the care of Mr. Prima and some of the other men and ran back to the barricade. "Keep it up, Connie! You're doing great! Don't stop till I tell you!"

Ms. Smithers and Ms. Nesselrode leaped from their seats and hastened over to where he stood. Ms. Smithers tugged at his shirt. "Oh, please don't let her keep running! She has no business running fifteen miles—"

"You've got no faith," he protested. "I tell you, she's gotten her second wind. She could run *thirty* miles if she wanted to."

And it did seem to be true. When she began her tenth mile, the whole crowd was on its feet yelling encouragement.

To make a long story short, and to save you the breathlessness that just about ruined us all, Ms. Cromwell not only ran fifteen miles but did an extra one for good measure. Her total time for the sixteen miles was 116 minutes, an average of seven and one-quarter minutes per mile. Mr. Wilhelm, who knows about these things, said that was phenomenal. I believe it. What was even more phenomenal, though, was the fact that Coach Greenlief was waiting for her at the finish line, a humbled and appreciative convert. As he reached out to shake her hand, she collapsed gratefully into his arms, and a new athletic alliance for Shad High School was born right there before our very eyes.

14

The famous race and reconciliation was followed by two days of celebration, the likes of which Shad had never known before. Most of it was viewed by the entire nation, thanks to the miracle of network television and its zealous reporters. That night there was a great bonfire on the school grounds and a barbecue in the cafeteria. Blue Grass music filled the crisp autumn darkness, and all the children got to stay up late. The older people carried posters and banners that said things like "It's 'In' to Be Old" and "Old Is Beautiful." Ms. Cromwell got several rides around the town square on various sets of shoulders while everyone sang "For She's a Jolly Good Fellow."

The next day—Sunday—with the unanimous agreement of the town's ministers, religious services were held in the school auditorium. At the end of the service the Reverend Mr. Hawkes got up and made a little speech. He said Shad celebrated its Three Ladies and their friends, who had brought new life and vitality to the community, and who gave people everywhere new hope that it is possible to live with meaning to the very end of one's days. It was a fine speech. When the Reverend Mr. Hawkes sat down, everyone applauded, even though you aren't usually supposed to clap in church.

That afternoon when the time arrived for the visiting friends to depart, the sky was beginning to cloud over and a chill wind blew off the river. The atmosphere at the Old Focus Home was not exactly gloomy, but there was a sort of wistful sadness touching everything.

"Well, now," Ms. Smithers said as they gathered on the front porch, "it's not as if we shall never see each other again—after all, you have to come back for the dedication ceremony. Now that you've seen the Home and Shad, it's going to be very difficult for you to stay away from us!"

Mr. Hatchett smiled fondly at her. "That's true, my dear, but we have commitments in our own communities."

"True," said Mr. Willis with a twinkle in his eye. "And if we left *there* to come *here,* it would create large holes in six different cities. Besides, such a concentration of power in one spot couldn't be good for the atmosphere. Shad might explode!"

"Such arrogance!" Ms. Cromwell snorted, slapping his arm. "But of course you're right."

After hugs all around, the six guests left, led by Ms. Staley on her motorcycle. Ms. Smithers, Ms. Nesselrode, and Ms. Cromwell watched until they were out of sight, then used the handkerchiefs they had been waving to wipe their eyes.

"You have *super* friends," I said, feeling a little sad myself. "I'll be glad when they come back for the dedication ceremony."

"You know, this may sound strange—but I feel as though we've already had the dedication ceremony," Ms. Nesselrode mused.

"Bosh!" Ms. Cromwell clutched at her chest. "The *real* ceremony will make these past two days look pale by comparison. Pray we all survive!"

Ms. Smithers didn't say anything. The tears kept well-ing up and spilling over until finally Ms. Cromwell asked, a bit impatiently, what her problem was.

"Nothing." Ms. Smithers sniffled and blew her nose. "It's just that this weekend was so perfect. I always get uneasy when things go well."

"There's no reason why they shouldn't continue to go well," Ms. Cromwell said. "It's all in the mind. You should do three laps around the block, Ernestine, to purify your thinking!"

The new truce between Ms. Cromwell and Coach Greenlief brought about fast and remarkable changes in the athletic program of Shad High School. For one thing, we girls were allowed to practice indoors, and not a minute too soon. November weather had set in for good, and the outdoor court was cold and blustery. Although our season wouldn't start officially until after Thanksgiving, arrangements were made for us to play several practice games with teams from neighboring schools. Despite our lack of experience, we won more often than we lost, thanks to Ms. Cromwell's effect upon the opposition. Mr. Prima and the Coach tried to talk us into trading our 1932 gym suits for more conventional wear, but Debbie and I convinced them that our uniforms were a vital offensive weapon.

After the Great Race and the renown it brought to the Home, Dad's life became terribly busy. In addition to wrapping up plans for the dedication, he was called on to speak before civic clubs and church groups. Delegations of people with a special interest in the elderly came to look at the Home. Dad reveled in the publicity. He also became rather persnickety about the house staying in order, so many visitors were dropping by. It got so I had to lock my room if I wanted any peace and quiet, or if I didn't want to make up my bed.

Ms. Nesselrode came bouncing into the lobby late one afternoon just before dinner, waving a letter aloft. "He's going to do it—Dr. Burney is going to have the Symphony perform my *New Symphonic Concertoratorio!*"

It was about as close to squealing as she had ever come in my presence. Ms. Cromwell and Ms. Smithers jumped from their chairs and joined her in a little ring-around-a-rosy in the middle of the room.

"That's terrific!" I said. "Isn't it, Dad?"

He peered at them over the top of his newspaper as though he did not approve of such behavior in people their age. "Yes, of course. Very nice." Fortunately the ladies did not notice his stuffiness, or if they did, they didn't let it bother them.

"He says I should play the piano solo," Ms. Nesselrode announced when they had finally collapsed to catch their breath. "As soon as I finish transcribing the instrumental parts, the Symphony is going to begin rehearsals. Imagine! I shall have to come out of retirement."

"It's only fitting," said Ms. Smithers. "You never really retired anyway. This can be your Commencement performance."

"Wouldn't it be wonderful if it could be performed here in Shad?" Ms. Nesselrode's eyes became starry. "Perhaps we could plan a Spring Arts Festival and invite—"

Dad thrust the newspaper aside. "Please! Think what that would mean in terms of numbers of people! An entire orchestra. A choral group. All those who would come to listen. There simply isn't room in Shad to accommodate that sort of crowd."

The stars in Ms. Nesselrode's eyes faded. She became her practical self once more. "You're right, of course, Stephen. Thank you for bringing me to my senses."

I didn't like it that Dad had squelched the idea. For a former dreamer, he certainly had done a complete turnabout. He hadn't had a get-rich-and-famous-quick scheme in weeks. These days anything he invested effort in had to be reasonable, sensible, and possible. I thought that was what I had wanted, but now that it had come to pass, I wasn't so sure anymore. A little daydreaming never hurt anyone.

"Well, anyway." Ms. Nesselrode yawned and rubbed her eyes. "I hope I shall finish soon. These long hours of transcribing little bitty notes on manuscript paper are hard on my old eyes. I expect I shall have to go to the doctor soon and have my glasses changed."

"We should all go," said Ms. Smithers. "In fact, I think I shall call the ophthalmologist in Ferris tomorrow and make an appointment for the three of us."

"*I* don't need my eyes checked," Ms. Cromwell protested. "I can see as well as ever!"

"Then why do you hold your book so far away from your face when you read?"

"Humph!" Ms. Cromwell said. "Isn't dinner about ready?"

"Quit trying to change the subject, Connie. Even if you can run sixteen miles in less than two hours, that's not going to help your presbyopia."

"What, pray tell, does my religion have to do with it?"

"Presbyopia is farsightedness, Constance," Ms. Nesselrode said tactfully.

"Well, speaking of running, who's going to jog with me after dinner has settled?"

Ms. Smithers and Ms. Nesselrode exchanged amused looks but they said no more about eye examinations. Ms. Smithers said it was too cold to run after dark, and Ms. Nesselrode insisted that she must work on the composition. I said I had already run two miles and had to do my homework. Ms. Cromwell turned to Dad.

"Perhaps you would like to run, Stephen?"

"No. I'm expecting a group from Virginia tomorrow. They're to call tonight to let me know when they'll arrive. I don't want to be away from the telephone."

"Stephen, don't you think it would be wise to cut down on these visits from all sorts of groups and delegations? It seems to me you never have fun anymore. You spend all your time advertising the Old Focus Home. You really don't have to do that on our account, you know. We're more than happy with the way you've managed. We'd like for you to have a life and identity that is separate from the manager's job—"

"You don't understand," Dad interrupted. "Do you realize what a revolutionary concept the Old Focus Home is?"

"Well, of course we do! We're the ones who thought of it."

"Ah, yes—but thinking of it and making it work are two different things. Someone has to iron out all the little practical problems and details—create a system that functions. Reubella, why are you looking at me like that?"

I didn't know I had been looking at him in any particular way, but then I realized my face was screwed into a horrendous frown. "I was just trying to . . . understand what you were saying."

"Well—do you?"

"I guess so."

The ladies were very quiet, but Dad didn't notice, because he went right on talking.

"The revolutionary part is the idea of choosing ahead of time the people you want to live with to the end of your days. Then, of course, the idea of pooling resources to provide housing and creature comforts. I get letters and calls every day—mostly from people who plan to start their own Homes. They want to come and see how we've remodeled the house. They're interested in the legal arrangements and so forth. I couldn't possibly turn them down even if I wanted to—which I don't."

"Strange," said Ms. Nesselrode. "Don't they want to talk to us?"

"Well, naturally I tell them about you—about your interests and your energy. But—no. I haven't had any direct requests for interviews with you."

There was a long silence, then Ms. Smithers said gently: "Stephen, there are two very important ingredients that people need to know about which have little to do with remodeling and legal arrangements."

"Oh?"

"Yes. One is Friendship. Only deeply loyal friends are able to endure each other's whims and peculiarities—and to enjoy each other's successes—and to weep at each other's griefs and failures. You can't live with just anyone, especially not someone you pick up at the last minute. You must begin early in life to cultivate those kinds of friends."

"And the other ingredient is Growing," Ms. Nesselrode added. "At our age the body is dying—more cells are perishing than are being replaced. But the mind and spirit can be replenished to the last. One needs to learn how it is done."

Dad waved one hand vaguely in the air. "Sure, I know. But that's something people have to work out for themselves. I'm certainly not going to deliver a sermon to every person who shows up here."

The ladies looked at each other. "Perhaps you should refer them to one of us," Ms. Cromwell said.

"I don't think that is necessary. Besides, each of you is so busy it seems a shame to bother you when I can answer their questions. It's my job, you know." He glanced at his watch. "I believe dinner is ready now. Let's not keep Hazel waiting."

After dinner the three ladies excused themselves, Ms. Cromwell to run, the others to go to their rooms and work. Their absence made the downstairs seem cavernous. Dad scribbled memoranda in his notebook, made some phone calls, and then took up the newspaper again.

I studied his face as he read and suddenly saw him as an old man in his seventies or eighties. Who would he choose to live with? Or more to the point, who would choose him? He had no friends that I knew of. He had no particular interest in sports or art or music or people, or in anything else that I could name. It was a chilling thought. Ms. Smithers and Ms. Nesselrode had sat right there and told him, and he hadn't even heard!

He looked up and caught me eyeing him. "Reubella, I feel like a specimen under a microscope. What is it? Do my feet smell bad or something?"

"No, sir."

"Then do me a favor and quit staring. Your eyes are burning holes in me!"

He laughed, but that didn't hide his irritation. I went back to my social studies project, but I couldn't concentrate. I kept thinking about Dad being a lonely old man, and how scary it was that a person could be right in the middle of a revolution and not be changed by it at all.

15

A few days later the three ladies boarded the Buxty Hooda and went to Ferris to see the eye doctor. When Ms. Cromwell said she was only going for the ride, Ms. Smithers winked at me. I kept my face straight.

The dedication ceremony was only a matter of days away. I couldn't wait. I didn't care all that much about the dignitaries and celebrities, but the friends of our ladies were going to return. They would stay with us through Thanksgiving. We had planned a huge turkey dinner with all the trimmings—the first of my entire life. Whenever I thought of it, I could hardly keep my mind on such everyday things as algebra and basketball practice. Thanksgiving for Dad and me had always been a bleak sort of day, with no special celebration and certainly no special meal. This time it was going to be different. I couldn't believe my good fortune.

Thanksgiving was on my mind as I checked the cinnamon rolls in the oven that evening. It was already dark outside, but the ladies had not returned from Ferris. A bright fire burned in the lobby fireplace. Hazel had left everything ready for dinner, so we were going to have the house to ourselves for a change after days of drop-in guests and delegations. The elegant aroma made my stomach growl in a most unseemly way. Impatient to eat, I was about to suggest to Dad that we not wait any longer when the front door opened and closed. I danced out of the kitchen and nearly knocked a bowl of salad off the sideboard.

"Well, thank goodness you're here at last! I was about to starve. Dinner's ready and—" The words froze on my tongue. The three people standing there were Ms. Nesselrode, Ms. Smithers, and Ms. Cromwell all right, but something terrible had happened. They were holding on to each other as though they feared they might fall. The brightness that usually danced in their eyes had been replaced by something dark. They looked *old.*

"Wh-what is it?" I asked.

"Hello, dear," Ms. Smithers said wearily. "Perhaps we could just sit a moment by the fire before dinner— would that be all right?"

"Sure!" I frenzied around, plumping up pillows on the chairs. "I could make some hot tea. Would you like some hot tea?"

"That would be lovely." Ms. Nesselrode looked grateful. "If it isn't too much trouble."

Out in the kitchen I put on water for tea and arranged the tray with cups, hardly knowing what I did. I was afraid. Whatever had happened had transformed them suddenly from gold coaches to withered pumpkins.

When I came back they were sitting exactly as I had left them—no chattering, no acting out the events of the day, nothing but silence as they stared into the fire. The tracks of tears marked Ms. Cromwell's cheeks. Ms. Smithers made occasional sniffling noises. I set the tea tray on the table in front of the fire.

"Did—did somebody die?"

Three pairs of eyes turned in my direction.

"We've had some rather troubling news, Reubella,

He rubbed his hand along the side of his face as though it pained him.

"But what about *our* Old Focus Home?" I asked.

"The sooner the ladies wake up to reality, the better. In a few days, when Ms. Nesselrode has had time to get over the shock, I'll sit down with them and give it to them straight. I'm *not* going to manage a nursing home—I don't want them to count on that. They've got to come up with another plan for themselves."

"But, Dad . . . we're their family!"

"Where did you get that idea? What we have between us is strictly a business arrangement—that's all. I have the signed contracts to prove it."

"No, that's *not* all! They've been like my own grandmothers. Look what they've done for us—and look what they've done for the town. They *belong* here."

"It was business. I made that clear from the beginning."

I sprang from the chair. The fire blurred orange through my tears. "Don't you have any feelings about anyone? No—don't even *answer* that! I *know* the answer. I've known it almost since I was born. You don't care about anybody unless they are useful to you! Good night!

"And I hope you can't sleep!" I yelled back as I stumbled up the stairs, wiping my nose with the back of a sleeve.

16

When you read in books about people who are plunged into despair, it sounds like a fast trip straight down into a dark hole. Well, that is what it is, let me tell you! First, the ladies called off the dedication ceremony, despite all my pleading. Not that I cared so much about the ceremony, but I had put a lot of store by their friends being with us for Thanksgiving dinner. Dad didn't put up any argument—I suppose he reasoned that not dedicating the Home would make it easier to dissolve the agreement when the time came. He promptly set to work sending letters to all the people who had been invited, telling them to forget it. I entertained notions of offering to take the letters to the post office and then tossing them into the town dumpster so they'd never be delivered, but that scheme never got beyond the notion stage. It is hard for me to be sneaky, even for a good cause.

Monday afternoon Ms. Cromwell didn't show up for basketball practice and didn't bother to call to say why. When I got home, worried almost to death, I found her in the rock room on the floor, poring over a book on snails and other mollusks. She was wearing a new pair of black-rimmed spectacles that made her dark eyes appear owlish.

"A fascinating book, Reubella—you should read it sometime. Reading is so much pleasanter since I've gotten these glasses—"

"Are you all right?" I interrupted. "We waited and waited for you!"

She looked at me blankly for a few seconds, and then her mouth dropped open. "Basketball practice! Oh, my goodness, Reubella—it completely slipped my mind!" She scrambled to her feet and began pulling on her sweater.

"No need to get yourself in a swit," I said. "Everyone went home."

She chastised herself for the rest of the afternoon, stomping about slapping her forehead and muttering, "How could I have forgotten? What's the matter with me?" until I went off to Prebble's Point just to get away.

She showed up for practice the next day, but for the first time in years she didn't run her usual two miles. As the week wore on she complained openly of aching joints, and became remote and absentminded. Needless to say, it affected our team performance.

"She sure isn't herself, is she?" Debbie observed. We were treating ourselves to a milk shake at Bagley's after a particularly disastrous practice session.

I shook my head. "No—and neither are the others. Can you believe that Ms. Smithers has let her hair go *gray?* And when her students come for art lessons in the middle of the day, she's upstairs sleeping!"

"What about Ms. Nesselrode?"

"She never even goes in the music room anymore! The piano's locked. She took the Concertoratorio solo to JoAnne Preddy last Sunday afternoon and mailed the rest of the score to the Symphony conductor. Since then she's mostly been sitting in her room, looking out at the river."

Debbie was sympathetic. "I don't see how you stand it."

"I'm not doing a very good job," I confessed. "It's like living full time at a funeral parlor."

"What does your dad say?"

"Nothing much." I didn't tell her that he and I were hardly speaking. I was ashamed for her to know that just any time now my own dad was planning to tell the three ladies that he was through with the Old Focus Home. Debbie has a strong sense of justice. She doesn't believe in hitting people while they're down.

"Well, you'll have to do something drastic," she said.

"Me? What can *I* do? They need dynamite, or maybe a thunderbolt!"

"Remember when Ms. Cromwell raced Coach Greenlief, and all her friends came down for the event? Call them up and tell them they have to come again, for emergency reasons."

"That wouldn't work. The ladies said they didn't want their friends to come now. That's why they canceled the dedication ceremony."

"Well, then, what about *one* of the friends?"

"You don't ever give up, do you?" I chewed the end of the plastic straw. "Which one?"

"The little guy that drives the yellow car," she said promptly.

I pondered. "Mr. Willis? Yes, probably he would— but I wouldn't ask him to come down. Maybe just get some advice."

"Whatever." Debbie sucked noisily at the last thick drops of milk shake and got up to leave. "But do *something!* The girls basketball team won't amount to anything if your ladies don't get it together."

"*My* ladies!"

She grinned. "Sorry. *Our* ladies, God bless 'em!"

I found Mr. Willis' address and phone number written

in Ms. Nesselrode's firm hand on the inside back cover of the telephone directory. Ordinarily I would have had problems getting the phone to myself, but since the previous Saturday evening the ladies had stopped sitting in the lobby to read and chat. When Dad went out to the post office after dinner, I dialed Mr. Willis' number. He answered on the second ring. "Emmanuel Willis speaking."

"Mr. Willis, this is Reubella Foster. Do you remember me?"

"Of course I remember you! How are you? And how is Holly? And Connie? And Ernestine? And your father?"

"That's what I was calling about."

"What's the matter?" His voice went from cheerful to serious.

"Well, it's kind of a long story," I said, sorry to be telling him the news over the telephone. Probably Ms. Nesselrode would be angry with me if she knew. "I'm not sure I can afford to tell you the whole thing long distance, but I'll give you the gist."

I told him about the eye examination and about the likelihood Ms. Nesselrode would lose her sight. I told him about her not being able to play in the premiere performance of *The New Symphonic Concertoratorio*. I told him about the slump all three of the ladies had fallen into. He was very quiet all the time I talked except for a stricken "Oh, no!" when I mentioned Ms. Nesselrode's eyes.

"Things are in a serious state around here," I finished. "The ladies just can't seem to get hold of themselves, and I don't know what to do. Mr. Willis, could you please come to Shad?"

I hadn't really known I was going to ask him to come, but I guess my insides decided he was needed in person.

"I'll be there by noon tomorrow," he said, not hesitating a minute. "And, Reubella . . . don't tell them I'm coming. I'll just happen by."

"O.K.," I said, "but don't forget your suitcase. You may have to stay a while."

"Yes, it sounds that way." He was silent for a moment, then he said, "When I got the letter saying the dedication ceremony had been called off, I thought they had gotten so involved in their six hundred activities that they didn't have time to dedicate the Home. I had no idea—"

"Yeah. Well, it sort of knocked the pins out from under them. And me. Always before they acted like nothing was too hard to overcome. It seems . . . they've given up."

Saying the words made me cold.

"Well, we'll just have to do something about *that*. I'll see you tomorrow, Reubella. And thank you for calling me."

I hung up the receiver and wiped my sweaty hands on the back of my jeans. Somehow things did not seem quite so hopeless, now that Mr. Willis was coming.

He arrived while I was at school, so I'm not sure what sorts of excuses he gave for happening by. I hope they were convincing, since Shad is not a place you pass through going to somewhere else. Nevertheless, by the time I got home he had settled in. I found him and the ladies in the music room. Somehow he had contrived to get Ms. Nesselrode to accompany him on the Steinway while he sang. For an old fellow he had a very nice tenor voice, although it cracked a little on the high notes. He hugged me, and I put on a pretty good act about being surprised to see him and all.

"He's going to stay!" Ms. Smithers beamed. "We talked him into staying."

Mr. Willis winked at me, and I tried not to grin. "That's good," I said. "Sure am glad you happened by."

That afternoon the ladies were in the best mood I had

seen them in for several days. I thought Mr. Willis could give himself a pat on the back for doing such a good job in such a short time, but he did not appear altogether elated. It was not until after dinner that I was able to get him to one side to find out how things were going.

"We have a problem, Reubella," he said, puffing his pipe. "They haven't told me a word about Holly's eyes. We're not going to get anywhere until one of them confesses."

"But I thought you were best friends! Best friends don't keep secrets from each other."

He looked over at me and smiled. "That's right. Do you have any good ideas about how to help best friends be straight with each other?"

I thought about it. "Yes, sir—but it will probably make the ladies mad at me. I'm chicken."

"Are you willing to risk it—for them?"

I thought about it some more. "O.K.," I said finally. "I'll do it. But I hope you'll be around to pick up the pieces afterward."

He patted my hand. "You won't be sorry. What's your plan?"

I told him. We went to the lobby, and he helped me build a fire in the fireplace.

You would almost think that nothing had ever happened, what with such a peaceful scene in the lobby that evening. I had my books spread out on the rug in front of the fire, and all the grown-ups were sitting around in the overstuffed chairs, talking. Dad had hauled out his pipe, too, and he and Mr. Willis were making the air blue with smoke rings. Everyone seemed so contented. I didn't want to start anything.

But Mr. Willis was counting on me. Besides, I couldn't keep my mind on my homework as long as I knew what had to be done. I took an enormous breath, exhaled, counted to ten, said my prayers, and said, "Ms. Nesselrode, have you told Mr. Willis about your eyes yet?"

If I had been Jove and had thrown a thunderbolt in the midst of the gathering, the effect could not have been more electric. The three ladies and Dad all looked at me. Dad's expression said I was an incredible busybody. Ms. Cromwell registered shock, Ms. Smithers surprise. Ms. Nesselrode looked reproachful, which was hardest of all for me to take. I closed my eyes so as not to see any of them.

"What about your eyes, Holly?" Mr. Willis asked gently. I opened mine again. To my relief everyone's attention had shifted to him.

"Well, it's . . . it's not anything for you to worry about." She fumbled for words. I felt terrible, like I had pushed her into an arena to fight before she was ready.

"Tell me," Mr. Willis urged.

The long-drawn-out silence filled the room into its far corners. I looked at the papers and books spread around me. The words on them wouldn't go into my brain. I wanted to be invisible or buried.

At last Ms. Nesselrode sighed, a tremendous giving-up kind of sigh. "Emmanuel, I didn't want to burden you with this."

He held up his hand. "Holly, would it be a burden to you if *I* had some personal problem that I needed to share with you because you are my friend?"

"Oh, no! Of course not! You know that I would want to know, and to do whatever I could—"

"All right, then. It works both ways."

She considered that, and then she nodded. "Yes. Forgive me."

At that point the flood gates opened. The ladies—all three of them—stumbled over each other's words to tell Mr. Willis about the visit to the eye doctor. They wept a lot. He prodded them about their activities and listened to their shamefaced confessions that they had begun to let things slide. They spoke of feeling fearful and despairing and helpless and discouraged. The more they talked, the less quavery their voices became. Suddenly, Ms. Cromwell stood up and flexed her muscles.

"Emmanuel, I am ashamed. We have been a bunch of silly geese! Do you remember that on the day of the race one of the banners read 'Old is not Dead'? Well, for the past week we have been living as though we did not believe it."

"That's true," Ms. Nesselrode agreed. "The Powers of Darkness have had hold of us for certain."

Ms. Smithers pulled at a loose strand of her fading hair and looked at it distastefully. "I have always thought of us as valiant—fighters to the last. How in the world did we give up so easily?"

"How indeed?" Mr. Willis smiled a little. "It may be that things were going so well for you here, you lost sight of the fact that you are mortal. It is true that we are dying, but we aren't dead yet."

"And it's wrong to give up until one cannot go another step," Ms. Cromwell spoke with her old firmness.

"Absolutely!" Ms. Smithers echoed. "Heavens—I must get on the telephone first thing tomorrow morning and round up my students. We're planning a showing in December. Whatever must they think of me, fuzzing about like this all week?"

Ms. Nesselrode wasn't saying very much. Mr. Willis went over and sat beside her.

"I shall have to change my way of doing things, Emmanuel—and that won't be easy."

"That's true enough, Holly. But the opposite of composing is not *de*-composing. You may lose your sight but not your vision. Your mind and spirit are sound, and you have a great deal of wisdom to share. You'll simply have to begin a new career."

Ms. Nesselrode actually giggled. "At my age?"

"And what's wrong with your age?" Mr. Willis drew himself up. "Remember, it's my age too. I'll thank you not to cast aspersions!"

The four old people laughed together, and the air seemed washed with their relief and new hope. Some tightness in my chest came loose, and I could breathe once more. I began gathering up my books and papers.

Dad scowled at me. "Reubella, you owe Ms. Nesselrode an apology."

But don't you see? I wanted to say. Everything is better now. They will be themselves again.

He turned to Ms. Nesselrode. "I don't suppose I can make her apologize, but I can tell you I didn't bring her up to meddle in other people's business. I'm sure if she were a little more sensitive to your feelings, she wouldn't have been so presumptuous."

"It's all right, Stephen," Ms. Nesselrode said gently. "I'll admit it took my breath at first, but only because I was hiding in such a cowardly way. I rather think Reubella did us all a great favor. Secrets separate friends. I am very grateful to you, my dear, for making me be honest with Emmanuel."

"Yes," said Mr. Willis. "She could have washed her hands of the entire business and let us go on fooling ourselves and each other. Personally, I'm glad she stuck her neck out for us."

"She has kept our feet on the ground during our weeks here in Shad," Ms. Cromwell said. "She has saved us from folly more than once."

"And I, for one, love her for it!" Ms. Smithers looked at me with such fondness that I feared my eyes were going to fill up in spite of everything. I was not used to such outspoken affection.

Dad was not particularly happy about their testimonials, but he covered it up. I suppose he feared that I would try such tactics more often if it got me pats on the back.

He did not know what a basic coward I was.

Mr. Willis stayed for two more days as a sort of resident comforter. "I'm glad the girls have you and your dad and this fine Home," he told me the morning he was to leave. It sort of startled me to hear him call them "girls" but I guess when he first knew them they *were* girls—and he was a boy. That whole train of thought distracted me for a moment. Then I realized what he had said.

"Well, I fear it is not as rosy as it looks," I said ruefully.

"What do you mean?"

I hesitated. It didn't seem fair to give him something else to worry about just as he was departing, particularly after he had done such a good job of restoring the ladies to their former condition. "Nothing. I was just referring to the fact that sometimes things happen that none of us are expecting. *You* know."

He gave me a probing look, but he didn't ask any more questions. He finished fastening his suitcase, and we went downstairs. After all the good-by hugging and kissing, he turned to Dad to shake hands.

"Thank you, Stephen, for taking such good care of them—they are very dear to me, you know."

Dad's look was inscrutable. "We try to make it comfortable."

The house seemed much larger with Mr. Willis gone. Ms. Cromwell looked about, as though trying to decide how best to fill the empty spaces. "Stephen," she said, "I notice that the swarms of visitors you used to squire about have diminished to practically nothing. Is it because you have taken our advice to slow down and enjoy life?"

"Yes." The answer came too quickly.

"That's wonderful! What will you do with your free time?"

"I . . . uh . . . haven't really decided yet. Maybe I'll start a Little Theater group in Shad."

The three ladies went into orbit. Ms. Cromwell's eyes gleamed. "How exciting! I used to do a bit of acting myself—you know I have a degree in drama."

"And costuming and stage design are two of my favorite pursuits." Ms. Smithers was beside herself. "What an opportunity for my art students!"

"I hope you intend to include musical comedy," said Ms. Nesselrode. "Several of my students are quite talented."

Dad saw his error. "Nothing is definite. I've only been thinking about it."

It wasn't true, of course. He and I both knew the only thing he was thinking about was telling them there wasn't going to be any more Old Focus Home.

"You aren't really going through with it after all this, are you?" I said when they were out of earshot. "Now that they are feeling so much better, how can you possibly get them all upset again?"

"Reubella, you have to quit playing God!" he shouted. "You haven't done anything but make matters worse. You've given them back their illusions. They imagine that from now on, it's all going to be hunky-dory!"

"It *could* be."

"No, it couldn't. And the sooner you get that through your head, the better off you'll be."

I looked at the hardness in his eyes and knew there was no use in arguing anymore. I couldn't swallow. When I spoke, the words came out thinly.

"All right, but please wait until after Thanksgiving. It's only a few days."

The ladies took new heart, and practically overnight the Old Focus Home was again like a huge hive, with dozens of people coming and going. The only difference was that there were no delegatiohs of observers wandering around in the halls, poking their heads in the rooms. After the gloom of the previous week, I welcomed the noise and confusion. Debbie, for her part, was downright smug about it!

Dad just sort of stayed out of the way, confining himself to answering the mail and the telephone and seeing that the household services were taken care of. He had gone from executive manager to maintenance man, biding his time until the Thanksgiving holiday was over.

Unfortunately, the ladies began to talk of rescheduling the dedication ceremony. Dad argued that it was too late —that the VIP's had already made their plans for the next six months and so forth.

"Then perhaps we can do it in the spring," Ms. Nesselrode suggested. "I think it would be lovely, when the new buds are out—"

"—and the birds will have returned," Ms. Smithers trilled, swooping about in her shabby caftan with her arms outstretched like bird's wings. "And we shall have weathered our first winter in the Old Focus Home."

"Tried by fire, you might say," murmured Ms. Crom-well.

Dad just shook his head and let them run on. As for me, I felt like a traitor by association. It is the same feeling as when you are standing over a bug and about to squash it, and you know that bug doesn't have the least idea of what is about to happen.

North Carolina weather is strange and wonderful. Other places in the United States you can more or less expect the seasons to do what they're supposed to. If you live in New England, for instance, you sort of know that once the first snow falls, it's going to be winter from then on, with days of snow and grayness and cold. But in North Carolina you can never predict the weather more than a few hours in advance. From late October on, it will be colder than an ice floe one week, with the air so hard it practically rings. Then the next week will be balmy, with seventy-degree days, and all the shrubs will be fooled and start to put out leaf buds. Then there will be days of rain and wind, followed by days of clear blue sky. And once in a while there will be a season of snow. If you put a great premium on consistency, this is no place to live, but if you love surprises, you will not be disappointed.

We had one of those balmy breaks in the weather the week of Thanksgiving, just when you would expect the days to be at their dreariest. Novembers in the eastern part of the state can be awfully bleak. After the trees have shed their leaves, the landscape sort of settles into a brownness for the duration of winter. School was to be out Thursday and Friday. I had more or less resigned myself to a small celebration. At least we would have the three ladies and a turkey, which is more than I have ever had on other Thanksgivings. But even though I looked forward to four free days, I dreaded what would come afterward. It was as though the good and bad were so mixed up, you couldn't have one without the other.

When Ms. Cromwell and I came home after basketball practice on Tuesday, Ms. Smithers met us at the door, her hair its old flaming orange again.

"Guess what?" she greeted us. "The Reverend Mr. Hawkes is lending us his houseboat for an excursion!"

"How splendid!" Ms. Cromwell exclaimed. "When do we leave?"

"Why not Thanksgiving Day? We'll have Hazel cook the turkey tomorrow, and we'll take it with us. Just think —Thanksgiving on the river. What a spectacular way to celebrate!" Ms. Smithers twirled around the lobby and came to a sudden stop in front of me. "What do you think of that, Reubella?"

"I . . . I guess I have to let it sink in first."

"I don't think we should make definite plans until we find out what Reubella would like," Ms. Nesselrode said from the doorway. "It's her Thanksgiving too."

"What about Dad? What does he say?"

The three ladies exchanged looks. They gathered around me and spoke in hushed tones. "I rather think your father is troubled about something, Reubella. He isn't himself," Ms. Smithers said. "That's one reason we thought the excursion would be a good idea—he needs to get away."

"We haven't actually spoken to him about it," Ms. Nesselrode added. "We thought if we could present it to him as an accomplished fact—"

"—that he couldn't resist, especially if he didn't have to do the work to get ready," finished Ms. Smithers.

What could I say? If I told them what was troubling him, all their good cheer would vanish. Thanksgiving would be like a funeral day. "Well, if Dad says O.K., it's fine with me," I said at last, giving up my dreams of a large meal around the dining room table with a huge turkey in the middle.

To my undying surprise, he didn't put up any sort of argument at all. "All right—I'm game," he said when Ms. Cromwell told him the plan. "Just so you don't dump all the arrangements in my lap."

"Never fear!" Ms. Smithers pointed a bent finger toward the ceiling. "All you have to do is board the boat, and perhaps be ship's captain once we're under way. We'll look after provisions and all."

And so it was decided. Once I got into the spirit of things, I was glad that we had given up the conventional dinner for this trip down the river. I had never been on a houseboat before. We scurried around packing sleeping bags and extra blankets and sweaters while Dad sought instructions from the Reverend Mr. Hawkes on the fine points of running the boat.

We spent Wednesday afternoon and evening loading the houseboat so that we could get the earliest possible start next morning. The weather continued to hold fair and warm. I took that as a good sign. I hadn't seen Dad so animated since before the race. He talked about the boat a lot, explaining how it could be run from either below deck or above. My spirits lifted. Perhaps he had changed his mind about the Old Focus Home—maybe he would be willing to hang in there until Christmas at least, especially if we had a lot of fun on this expedition.

Thanksgiving morning, just as dawn broke, we pulled away from the marina dock. I felt like Columbus or somebody. Ms. Smithers surprised us by hauling a large bottle of champagne from her reticule.

"I know you're supposed to do this sort of thing before casting off, and the crew doesn't do the christening, but if you'll pardon the expression, 'any old port in a storm.' This is to declare that we are on the First Annual Thanksgiving Houseboat Expedition, sponsored by the

Old Focus Home of Shad, Inc. May this tradition continue for as long as any of us is able to navigate!" And raising the bottle aloft, she brought it crashing down across the blunt bow, sending a froth of champagne into the morning breeze. All of us clapped and cheered except Dad, who busied himself with some ropes at the other end of the boat.

Later as he leaned against the rail looking downriver through Ms. Cromwell's binoculars, I went and stood beside him, inhaling the comforting smell of his leather jacket and the pipe-tobacco odor that always lingered around him.

"Thanks for saying we could take this trip," I said. "I didn't think you would."

He lowered the binoculars and looked at me. "Well, I thought it would be easier to tell them when we got home again if they had this holiday to remember."

"But that's a dirty trick—getting them all softened up and then—whammo!"

He shook his head. "I don't think so. It seems kinder than just bringing up the subject like a bolt from the blue."

I pondered what he said and had to allow that it made sense. After a while I asked, "What're you going to say?"

"I don't know yet. I thought perhaps this experience together would help me know what to say."

For some reason I couldn't be angry with him even though I was miserable about what was going to come. He sounded different—quiet, and right on the edge of sad.

That day was glorious. The temperatures climbed into the mid-seventies and hung there. We stayed on deck most of the time, shedding our sweaters and jackets. The gulls flew at our stern, dipping and diving to pick off the fish that the boat's engine churned up. Ms. Cromwell womanned the outside wheel wearing a faded captain's hat that she claimed was a relic from her year on an icebreaker in the Arctic. Ms. Smithers relished the sunshine so much that she scarcely moved out of the deck chair all day.

"I want it to soak into my bones," she said. "Perhaps they won't crackle and pop so much this winter."

Ms. Nesselrode had to wear dark glasses and a wide-brimmed straw hat to protect her eyes, but she drank in the sounds and smells. She especially loved the rhythmic motion of the houseboat. "Ah, how I wish I had taken this trip before I finished the Concertoratorio," she said regretfully. "There is so much music out here!"

"Well, for goodness' sakes, Holly—you must leave some music for other people to write!" Ms. Cromwell fussed. "Can't you ever be satisfied?"

Dad went about quietly, relieving Ms. Cromwell at the wheel when she showed signs of fatigue, or bringing Ms. Smithers a cool drink, or describing for Ms. Nesselrode the scenery along the shore which she could not see well.

Sunset was a spectacular, silent blaze reflected in the foamy wake. Dad cut the engine and we drifted along, aware of the soft sounds of water lapping against the sides and birdcalls from the woods on the near shore.

"About time to moor for the night," he said. "Tomorrow, if the weather holds, we'll go to where the river flows into the sound, and then head back to Shad."

"I wish we could go on like this forever," I said. "I'll bet we could go clear around the world."

"True, but we might have a little problem navigating the Cape of Good Hope in this houseboat," Ms. Cromwell said. "It isn't built for stormy seas."

Dad brought us in to shore and tied up at a long pier where there were no other boats. The pier belonged to one of the cottages along the Peaceful that was vacant in winter. The five of us went belowdecks and prepared our meal of warmed-over turkey and dressing, cranberry

sauce, and rice in the tiny combination galley and sleeping quarters. We laughed and joked, examined the cupboards, and exclaimed about the little refrigerator. The
bunks lining the walls served as seats. We all sat cross-
legged on them, close and snug once more as we had
been that evening in early fall when the ladies first came
to live with us. Suddenly, in spite of the warmth and the
good smells I felt very sad. This was the end of it. We
would never be close like this again.

"Stephen, dear," said Ms. Nesselrode, "I can never
thank you enough for this wonderful excursion."

"Nor I," said Ms. Smithers. "It is the most satisfying
fun I have had in recent years."

"I don't like to get sentimental," Ms. Cromwell said
gruffly. "However, I must say, Stephen, that you have
been more like a son to me than my own son, who is far
away from here."

I sat up a bit straighter. Ms. Cromwell had a *son?*

The other two nodded. "It has been a long time since
the three of us have had family that we could claim," said
Ms. Nesselrode. "Until coming to Shad I had almost
forgotten what it felt like."

Dad fussed around the small stove, stirring the rice
that didn't really need stirring. He kept his back to us.
"Yes, well." His voice sounded muffled. "I'm . . . glad
that you've enjoyed the trip. A little vacation never hurt
anyone."

We ate our Thanksgiving dinner in silence. I kept
sneaking looks at Dad. Were his eyes red, or was it my
imagination? I finally decided it was from being out in
the sun all day with no sunglasses on.

We spread our sleeping bags on the bunks and turned
in early. The three ladies settled into a chorus of snoring
that alarmed me at first, but then was just funny. I lay in
the dark listening and wondered whether, if Ms. Nesselrode could hear this, she would include it in her Concert-

oratorio. The thought tickled me till I finally had to turn over and bury my face in the pillow so no one would hear me giggling.

I don't remember going to sleep, but suddenly I was jarred awake by the furious rocking motion of the boat. Things were falling and banging about and my head felt as though someone had dislodged my brain. I propped on one elbow and waited for my eyes to get used to the darkness. It seemed that sitting up was pretty much out of the question. Since I didn't hear any more snoring, I figured that the others were awake too. "Hey, what is this?" I asked. "What's going on?"

"I . . . think it's a storm," Ms. Smithers quavered from the depths of her sleeping bag. "Stephen has gone up on deck to see that everything's properly fastened down."

I thought about Dad out there alone in the cold, windy darkness. Struggling out of my sleeping bag I groped for jeans and sweater, and dressed as fast as I could, considering the dark and the unrelenting motion of the boat. The cupboards had swung open and the canned goods stored there had fallen out all over the floor. I had to watch my step to keep from being thrown off balance by one of the rolling cans. Just as I was groping my way to the door, the refrigerator came open, casting an unexpected beam of light across the cabin floor.

"Reubella, do be careful!" Ms. Nesselrode sounded alarmed. "Your father wouldn't want you to go out there, I'm sure."

"I'll be careful. He shouldn't be out there by himself."

"You're right," said Ms. Cromwell's gruff voice. "You stay here—I'll go out there." She sat up in her bunk and attempted to get to her feet, but at that moment another can dropped from the cupboard over her and landed squarely on her head. With a little moan she fell backward on her bunk.

"Heavens!" Ms. Smithers was beside her in a flash.

"Connie, dear—are you all right?"

"Yes, I'm all right, darn it!" But she made no more attempts to get up. I closed the refrigerator door and the cabin was plunged in darkness, but as soon as I took my hand away, the door came open again.

"Now what!" I fussed, looking around for something heavy to lean against it.

"Take my parasol," said Ms. Nesselrode, pointing to where it hung on a hook in the corner. "Stick it through both handles."

I followed her orders, and the door remained shut. "All of you stay right where you are," I said. "Don't try to come out on deck for any reason whatever." Nobody, including Ms. Cromwell, gave me any argument.

The force of the wind against the door was so great that I had to lean all my weight to push it open. Once I did, the cold almost took my breath away. How could it have changed so quickly and drastically? The door clanged shut behind me, and I stood for a moment trying to get my bearings. The ledge was very narrow, and I had to hold on to the rail for dear life to keep from losing my footing. I listened hard to hear above the howling of the wind. Tears came to my eyes and my nose stung with the cold.

"Dad! Dad, where are you?" The words were swept away by the wind. The boat rocked and banged against the pier. One thing was certain, I was no help to anyone just holding on to the rail. I groped my way toward the bow—and met Dad head on coming around from the other side. Judging by the look on his face, I must have scared him to death.

"Reubella, what are you doing out here! Go back in the cabin, quick!"

"I came out to help you!"

"There's nothing you can do. I'm going to untie the ropes, and we're going out!"

"What? In this storm? Why can't we stay here?"

"The boat will be chewed up banging against the pier —and it's not doing the pier any good, either."

It didn't seem to be a terribly smart idea, but who was I to argue? Just then the rain began to fall in icy sheets.

"Go get Ms. Cromwell up and tell her to take the inside controls. As soon as I undo all the ropes I want us to shove off."

Too frozen to protest, I turned and went back to the cabin door, still gripping the rail. If getting out had been difficult, getting in seemed impossible. The wind held the heavy door shut, and my feet were too slippery to get a purchase on the narrow deck ledge. Finally I banged loudly, not really very hopeful that any of the ladies would be able to open it from the inside, but in desperate circumstances you try anything once. In a moment or two as I pulled with all my might, the door suddenly swung outward. I almost went over the railing. Hands grabbed me wherever they could get hold. I was hauled wet and dripping into the cabin by an ankle, a pocket, and one arm.

"Good heavens, child! What is it doing out there?" Ms. Cromwell started drying me off with a towel. Ms. Smithers and Ms. Nesselrode wiped the cabin floor where water had poured in the door.

"No time for that." I pushed the towel away. "Dad says for you to take the controls down here. He says we're starting back right now." I explained about the damage to the boat and the pier.

"It is sheer folly!" Ms. Cromwell said in no uncertain terms. "We would be navigating upriver against the current, and in this wind and rain."

"I tried to tell him, but—"

Ms. Cromwell was pulling on woolen slacks and a heavy jacket. She jammed the faded captain's hat on her head.

"You're not going out there," I said, but it was more of a question than a statement. "You'll be swept overboard!"

"I'll bet Stephen doesn't have a rope tied around his waist, does he?"

"No, ma'am—not that I could see."

She took a coil of rope that hung on a peg by the controls. "If Stephen is going to run a ship, he needs to learn how a captain takes care of himself," she said grumpily. Then without another word she pushed open the door and struggled out into the dark.

"How did she do that?" I pointed to the door. "I could hardly budge it!"

But Ms. Smithers and Ms. Nesselrode were too concerned about her safety to worry about how she got the door open. Ms. Smithers wrung her hands and bemoaned the fact that she was not strong enough to be of any use on deck.

"Then make yourself useful down here," Ms. Nesselrode said. "Put some water on to boil for tea. They'll be frozen when they come down. And I'm going to get these blankets ready so they can get out of their wet clothes."

Several minutes went by, and I became uneasy. One or the other of them should have been back by that time.

"I'm going out," I said, getting to my feet.

"No, darn it! I feel like Noah sending out doves!" Ms. Smithers fussed. "Only none of them is coming back."

In the end, though, they let me go, because they were worried too. The two of them helped me push the door open, and shortly I was on the slippery deck once more. I longed for mittens as I gripped the now icy railing and made my way around to the pier side of the deck. In the semidarkness I could make out two figures—one lying stretched out on the deck, the other bending over it.

I stumbled over, numb with cold and fright, praying

that the lying-down person wasn't dead.

Dad was the unlucky one. Ms. Cromwell seemed relieved to see me. "Come on, help me haul him down below. He fell overboard, and I think he hit his head against the pilings."

I was shaking so hard I don't know how I was any help at all, but between us we managed to drag him around to the other side. I banged on the door again. "Stand back," I panted. "The door can knock you winding!"

It seemed forever before we were all inside again, and the door was closed once more against the wind and rain. We laid Dad on the floor, and Ms. Cromwell and I flopped down beside him and tried to catch our breath. Ms. Nesselrode and Ms. Smithers scurried about the cabin, wiping up water and fetching blankets and dry clothes.

"I've . . . got . . . to . . . see . . . about Dad," I gasped when Ms. Nesselrode handed me jeans and shirt to put on.

"Get these on immediately!" she ordered. "It won't do any good at all for you to catch pneumonia. Ernestine will look after your dad."

Because of the rope tied around his waist, it took all of us working together to get his soggy coat and trousers off. There was a large purple lump at his temple and his face was badly scratched.

"He *did* have a rope," I said. "Thank goodness! He might have drowned."

"Yes," said Ms. Cromwell in a peculiar, flat voice.

We moved him from the wet spot on the floor where he had been lying and wrapped him in a blanket that Ms. Smithers had warmed in the oven. "Dad!" I called softly. "Can you hear me?"

It seemed forever before he finally began to make coming-to noises. "Got to get ropes undone," he mumbled and tried to get up.

"That's all taken care of," I lied. "Lie still. You've been hurt."

"Ms. Cromwell . . . start engine . . . Going back—"

She leaned close to him. "Everything is fine, Stephen. You needn't worry." That seemed to satisfy him, because he quit trying to get up. I signaled her to come with me to the smaller cabin which was behind the control room.

"Tell me what happened out there," I whispered. "How long was he overboard?"

"When I went on deck I tried to talk him out of getting under way during the storm, but he wouldn't listen to me. I did finally persuade him to tie the rope around his waist and secure the other end to the boat."

"You mean, he didn't have on the rope before you went out?"

She shook her head.

"Then—you saved his life!"

"Who knows?" she shrugged. "Perhaps if I hadn't been out there to distract him, he would never have lost his footing. But the boat lurched and threw him off balance. I was at the rail as soon as he went over. There was a real danger of his being crushed between the boat and the pier. I'm afraid I didn't haul him up very tenderly— time was of the essence."

I threw my arms around her and burst into sobs.

"Now, now, dear. It's quite all right. I don't think he has more than a mild concussion. The boat is still firmly moored, and we shall stay right here until tomorrow morning."

We sat up the rest of the night drinking hot tea and watching over Dad. The rocking and banging eventually subsided, and by morning the motion of the boat indicated that the storm had passed. When it became light enough, Ms. Cromwell and I went outside to survey the damage.

"This pier is built more solidly than your dad realized," she commented. "There are only a few splintered places where the boat bumped. Structurally it seems to be none the worse."

"What about the houseboat?" I said. "I guess Mr. Hawkes is wondering this very minute whether we're on the bottom of the sound."

"It's all right. But it wouldn't be if we had gone out in the river last night. Look!"

I followed her pointing finger with my gaze. The river was full of floating tree limbs, boats adrift, and other indiscernible pieces of trash that bobbed and floated in the current.

"Gosh—that must've been some storm!"

"Probably history-making. Wouldn't you just know that the five of us would pick a once-in-a-century storm to be out in?" She chuckled. "It will make a fine story!"

By the time we got back to Shad late that afternoon, Dad was sitting up. He had a splitting headache, though, and let Ms. Cromwell run things. He didn't have much to say, but I attributed that to the condition of his head.

The man who owned the marina seemed as glad to see us as we were to be safe in harbor again. "I was about to go call the Coast Guard when I seen you through my glass," he said as he helped us with the boat. "How'd you weather it? We ain't had a late-fall storm like this'n since I was a boy!"

Ms. Cromwell told him, more or less, how we had managed, although she left out the more heroic parts. She spoke at length about Dad's good sense in lashing us to a sturdy pier overnight. "If he hadn't," she concluded, "all of us—boat and people—would have been chewed to a pulp by all the flotsam in the river."

The man looked dubious as Dad emerged from the cabin supported by Ms. Smithers and Ms. Nesselrode, one on each side.

"Seasick, huh?" he commented.

"Of course not!" Ms. Cromwell was indignant. "He slipped in the worst of the storm and hit his head—in fact, he may have a skull fracture. We're taking him straight to the doctor this minute. We'll come back to unload the rest of our things after we're all rested up."

"Don't know whether you'll be able to find a doctor in Ferris on Thanksgiving weekend. Besides, how do you intend to get him there?"

"In our van. I left it parked on the street." She pointed.

"Is that there *your'n?* Lord, I thought it belonged to some hippies or somethin'! I was gonna see the constable about it if didn't anybody claim it before the mornin'."

"The constable would have told you to whom it belonged," she said loftily as we moved away. "His wife's on the track team that I coach."

18

It was close to midnight when we finally made it back to the Old Focus Home. I do not think I have ever seen a more welcome sight. The doctor in Ferris had prescribed rest and no excitement for Dad for the next few days. I decided to adopt the same prescription for myself, at least through the remainder of the holiday weekend.

"I'm going to sleep until noon tomorrow," I mumbled as we hauled our belongings inside.

"Let's *all* sleep until noon," Ms. Smithers said. "Oh, thank goodness for a warm, cozy place to come home to!"

"Amen and Amen!" echoed Ms. Nesselrode.

Ms. Cromwell didn't join in. She fussed with the strings on her duffel bag. Poor Dad was hardly listening. His face was drawn, probably from contending with the ache in his head.

"Go get ready for bed while I fix you some aspirin and hot tea," I ordered.

"Sorry to be so much trouble," he said weakly. "In a day or two—"

"It's no trouble," I said. I started to add "when it's someone you love," but changed my mind.

I brought a glass of water, two aspirin, a cup of tea, and

two of Hazel's famous cinnamon buns and sat in the chair beside his bed while he polished off everything except the napkin.

"Thanks," he said, with a huge sigh. "That was delicious—I didn't know I was hungry."

"And now, lights out." I removed the tray and took away one of the pillows at his head. "And remember, you aren't supposed to get up and do around in the morning —doctor's orders."

"Don't worry. I couldn't if I wanted to." He scrooched down under the covers, and I smoothed the blanket and spread.

"How does it feel, being tucked in by a fifteen-year-old?" I teased.

"Kind of nice," he murmured, his eyes already closing. "It's been a long time since I was tucked in by anyone. 'S the problem about growing up . . ."

His voice trailed off. I turned out the light and took the tray to the kitchen, pondering what he had said. Dad had tucked me in until I was eleven, when I told him to stop because I was too big for that. But since he didn't have a mother or a father, he had probably done without being tucked in from the time he was just a little guy. He probably hadn't gotten enough tucking in, the way I had. I felt sad for him, especially since it seemed too late in his life to do anything about it.

He stayed very quiet for the next couple of days, during which time he was ministered to by Ms. Nesselrode, Ms. Smithers, and Ms. Cromwell. They each had different specialties. Ms. Smithers was good at cold compresses on the forehead, overseeing the diet, and other soothing comforts. Ms. Nesselrode preferred reading to him, although she was limited by the condition of her eyes to only a short reading time each day. Luckily, she had memorized a lot of poetry and lines from plays when she was younger, so she could quote things without looking at books. Dad sometimes joined her in the play lines because he knew Shakespeare from his acting days. They had a good time prompting each other and discussing meanings and all.

Ms. Cromwell, being more restless than the other two, ran errands and gave orders to the household help. On Sunday afternoon she and I went down to the marina to unload the remainder of our belongings from the houseboat.

Inside the little cabin I kept remembering the bright Thanksgiving Day we had had together, and how Ms. Smithers had declared our excursion the First Annual. I could hardly bear to think about it.

"It was a lovely trip, wasn't it?" Ms. Cromwell said as she viewed the pile of blankets, boxes, and bundles on the cabin floor.

"Yes. It was the best Thanksgiving I ever had."

"H'mmm. Interesting coincidence. It was the best I ever had, too."

That astonished me, since Ms. Cromwell professed to be seventy-two years old and had been around the world more times than she could count. "Maybe whichever one you've just had is always the best," I said, "because its the one that's clearest in the mind."

She shook her head and shouldered one of the boxes. "No, many Thanksgivings of my life are very clear in my memory, but this was the best—no doubt of it."

I picked up the two sleeping bags and a blanket roll and followed her out of the cabin, hoping she would not ask me any questions until I could swallow the lump in my throat.

Thank goodness the basketball season got under way in earnest, because as Dad began to feel better, I began to get anxious again. For various reasons he had put off telling the ladies the Old Focus Home was washed up, but now there were no obstacles in his way that I could see. Waiting for him to do it made me as nervous as a spider under a dripping faucet. Having homework, basketball practice, and a tight game schedule probably kept me from breaking out with hives or something. Debbie must have thought I was slightly crazy during that time, but being the good friend she is, she resigned herself to doing a lot of listening.

"Christmas is almost upon us," Ms. Nesselrode said at dinner one evening. Her eyes twinkled. "Constance, you must drive Ernestine and me to Ferris. We have a bit of shopping to do!"

"Oh, yes!" Ms. Smithers clasped her hands in front of her. "Oh, *think* how wonderful Christmas will be this year—our first in the Home. Why, we shall probably have to declare our rooms off limits to Reubella and Stephen until all the wrapping is d—"

"I don't have time to take you," Ms. Cromwell said brusquely, cutting Ms. Smithers off. She picked up a piece of celery and bit it with a loud crunch. Ms. Nesselrode and Ms. Smithers exchanged puzzled glances, but no more was said about a shopping trip. I figured Ms. Cromwell was too preoccupied with getting our team through a winning season to be thinking about Christmas stuff.

It was probably just as well. The more of themselves the ladies invested in the Home, the harder it would be for them to leave. I looked at Dad, wondering for the hundredth time how I could find out what his intentions were without coming right out and asking. He, however, was concentrating absolutely on eating and seemed not to have heard a word of the conversation.

I didn't realize how uptight I was about the whole thing until one Saturday morning when I slept later than usual. I woke with a start and lay still for a few moments trying to figure out what had awakened me. No music from the music room, no bumping about on the stairs, no voices murmuring. Plainly, I woke up because there wasn't any noise! The house hadn't been that quiet in ages!

In a flash I was out of bed and in the hall, not even taking time to put on a robe. The doors to all of the unoccupied upstairs rooms stood open. I knocked on Ms. Nesselrode's door, then Ms. Smithers', and last on Ms. Cromwell's. No answer.

Don't panic, I told myself sternly. They're downstairs eating breakfast.

But the kitchen was empty—spotlessly clean and cold. For all of its looks the last meal might have been prepared weeks before. I raced to the front window and looked out. The Buxty Hooda was gone.

I'll admit that I went slightly berserk at that point. I ran around the house, calling everyone's name at the top of my lungs. I almost collided with Dad as he was coming in the back door.

"Have you already sent them away? Without even telling me? How could you *do* such a thing! It's so *sneaky* and *cowardly*—"

Dad looked at me as though I had lost my mind. "What are you talking about?"

"They're gone! You sent them away! Why couldn't you at least wait until I had told them good-by!"

By that time I was pounding his chest with both fists. He grabbed my wrists and held me still. "Reubella, for pete's sake, calm down! I haven't sent anyone anywhere. Just cool it!"

"Then where are they? You think you're so great, telling 'em behind my back! Well, you're not going to get away with it. If they go, *I* go! I'll leave this very day and you can't make me stay here!"

It is to Dad's credit that he did not slap my face. He continued holding my wrists until I sort of ran down, and then in a quiet voice he told me that the ladies had gotten up very early and had gone to Raleigh on business. They would be back that night after dinner. I don't know when I've ever felt so stupid and ashamed.

"I'm sorry," I mumbled, looking down at my bare feet.

"It's O.K." His voice was so kind that I dared to look at him. "I know you've been under a lot of strain lately—in fact, I'm surprised you haven't done more storming around than this."

If you would just let me know what you're going to do, I thought, but I couldn't for the life of me get the words off my tongue. If there was no hope, I didn't want to know about it. I am a coward too.

"Go upstairs and put on some clothes before you catch cold," he said. "I'll have your breakfast ready when you come down." That in itself was enough to boggle the mind—I don't know when Dad had last fixed my breakfast.

It was a long, waiting day. I did some chores, finished my homework, and then had nothing to do. Debbie had a Saturday job at Bagley's to earn Christmas money, so I went there and hung around a while. We couldn't talk, though, because of the customers. When I got home at four, the ladies still had not returned.

Dad and I ate warmed-over soup for supper. Afterward I read and he wrote letters. The mantel clock made great, brassy tocking sounds. The house creaked and murmured like the empty insides of some hungry animal. When at last I heard the chugging of the Buxty Hooda, my bones seemed to melt with relief. I knew then that I had not ever expected to hear it again.

Since the fateful evening when the three of them had come home bearing the burden of Ms. Nesselrode's failing sight, I had been leery of their daylong treks to other towns. Who could predict what their state of mind would be when they returned? Usually they were full of chatter and funny stories, but pessimist that I am, I always held my breath until I was sure everything was all right.

I suppose this particular evening I wanted them more than ever to be boisterous and funny, so when they came in quiet and calm, it frightened me.

"Gosh, I'm glad you're back!" My voice was too loud, but being pent up all day had taken its toll. While Dad went to fix a snack, I scurried about helping them with their wraps and asking senseless questions, as though all my noise and action could make everything normal again.

"Reubella, are you feverish?" Ms. Cromwell asked suddenly, giving me one of her looks.

"No, ma'am. I'm ... just glad to see you is all." I stood there feeling like an overgrown puppy that has just knocked over a vase from an excess of enthusiasm. I had never felt so large.

Ms. Cromwell smiled and patted my cheek, which was somewhat out of character for her. "How fine to be welcomed home so warmly!" Then her face became serious. "Actually, I'm glad you and Stephen are still up. We can tell you about our day."

"And about our decision," Ms. Nesselrode said, settling in her favorite chair before the fire.

"Decision? What decision?" Dad entered from the kitchen, bearing the tea tray. He set it on the table and looked warily from one to the other.

"Well," said Ms. Smithers, "you must understand that this is no lightly considered thing—we've been trying to make up our minds for ... for weeks."

"And you must realize, too, that it has been an extremely difficult decision to make because ... because—" Ms. Cromwell could not go on. She clamped her mouth shut and cracked her knuckles.

Ms. Smithers tried again. "Do you remember, Stephen, that once we talked about what made the idea of the Old Focus Home successful? We said then that the most important elements were Friendship and Growing. As I recall, we argued at the time that these were more important than legal arrangements or the Home's physical condition."

Dad nodded. "Yes, I remember. And I see now that you were right."

Ms. Cromwell blinked. "You do?"

I myself was astonished to hear his matter-of-fact concession. When had he changed his mind?

"That is not relevant just now," Ms. Nesselrode said, waving the moment aside. "What is more to the point is that there was another ingredient which belongs in the mix that we three overlooked. It was very dumb and shortsighted of us."

"What are you talking about?" I asked.

"The Home won't work if all the people who live in it are of the same generation. Period. It is one thing to have people of all ages participating in the activities of the Home, but I'm speaking of residents. We should have chosen younger friends who love us as much as our contemporaries do. We simply didn't do it. Not until I learned that I was going blind did it strike all three of us at once—eventually we will all be unable to care for either ourselves or each other. We are all the same age."

It was exactly the same conclusion Dad had reached weeks before. I looked at him. His face was a study.

"It seems rather late in time for us to regroup and do it differently," Ms. Smithers said. "Friendships take a long time—they have to be discovered and developed. We haven't time to search for younger friends, who would in turn search for friends younger than themselves. The true Old Focus Home should be like the traditional French pot-au-feu, simmering forever with new ingredients added each day."

"So, Stephen, we're leaving."

Ms. Cromwell's voice was like a cannon shot in the quietness. "We're going to enter a retirement home somewhere, before Holly's eyes get much worse. Probably we shall leave in January, but your salary as manager will continue through the year. You are to keep whatever furnishings we've bought for the house. There won't be room for them where we are going."

It was all happening too fast. My head spun.

"We are so sorry to break the faith with you this way," Ms. Nesselrode said quietly, looking sadly from Dad to me. "You have both been wonderful to us. Please understand that it is *our* failure and not—"

"No!" said Dad, so suddenly and so loudly that the four of us jumped. "I won't hear another word!"

"But, Stephen—"

"Not another word, I say! You are *not* leaving!"

I, of course, was truly dumbfounded. My first impulse was to leap up and down and scream joyously, but a sliver of doubt held me back. Why was Dad taking that position when they were offering to do exactly what he wanted? At least with them making the decision, he didn't have to look like the bad guy. Maybe he was holding out for money—a breach-of-promise settlement or something. I began to get furious. So help me, I wouldn't let him get away with it! I would tell the ladies and their lawyer and the world that he had meant to throw them out on their ears—

"Now *I* have a few things to say, so be quiet and listen." Dad's voice broke into my thoughts. He sounded almost as commanding as Ms. Cromwell. "I saw that the Old Focus Home wasn't going to work because there would be no one to care for you when you were very old and maybe ill—"

"—or blind," Ms. Nesselrode interrupted.

"—or blind. No one except me, that is, and I wanted no part of it. You couldn't *pay* me enough to do it. Who wants to be stuck with a bunch of old people who have to be waited on all day long?"

"Who indeed?" Ms. Smithers nodded in perfect agreement.

"I had every intention of informing you that, as of the end of the year, you must make arrangements to leave here."

"It appears that you were way ahead of us," Ms. Nesselrode said admiringly.

"There was just one problem," Dad went on. He got up from his chair and began pacing, his hands in his pockets. "I couldn't bring myself to do it. Every time I would start to tell you, I'd chicken out. I couldn't understand it—I'm not that decent a guy!"

"For shame, Stephen, talking about yourself that way!"

He waved his hand for Ms. Nesselrode to be quiet and let him finish.

"Then we went on that houseboat trip. Partly as a result of that I've concluded that I can't let you leave because . . . because—"

Here Dad became very agitated and red-faced. It seemed that the words he needed to say had lodged sideways in his throat and simply wouldn't come out.

"Because?" Ms. Smithers prompted, leaning forward in her chair.

"Because, darn it, I've become very fond of you three!" He turned his back on us and looked into the fire. In a softer voice he added, "In fact, I have come to love each of you."

The room was absolutely still except for the crackling of the fire and the ticking of the clock. The unlikely words Dad had uttered hovered around us like uncertain moths. Water kept filling my eyes and blurring the fire. I used the back of my hand to wipe them, but it didn't do much good.

194

"You are like three aspects of the mother I don't remember, but ever so much better friends than a mother would be. You've given Reubella and me the family we've never had. You've transformed the house—the whole town—from drab and commonplace to bright and alive. And then, of course"—he turned to Ms. Cromwell —"there is the matter of my life, which I owe you. Just tonight, waiting for you to return, I realized that we needed you far more than you will ever need us. I guess what I'm saying is, business matters aside, the Old Focus Home *will* work because you have Reubella and me for your younger friends—and family, if you will have us. I hope you won't leave."

"You really mean that, don't you?" Ms. Cromwell's eyes probed his.

Dad nodded.

The next minute he was practically smothered by the hugs of four doting females, one of whom—in case you haven't guessed it—was me.

Commencement

One morning in late March, Coach Greenlief showed up on our front porch with his baseball hat in his hand and a nervous expression in his eyes. He asked for Ms. Cromwell. First the two of them had a long, private conversation in the rock room. Then Ms. Nesselrode and Ms. Smithers were called in, and finally Dad. I noted all this with mounting curiosity from the top of a stepladder in the lobby, where I was washing windows as my contribution to spring cleaning. At length all five adults reappeared. Ms. Cromwell cleared her throat loudly.

"Reubella, with your consenting vote, we would like to accept as a full resident of the Old Focus Home our friend, Coach Greenlief. He has no family here and would like to be a part of ours."

In my astonishment I knocked over the bucket of vinegar water. For days afterward the lobby smelled faintly of pickles.

I voted yes.

So if you like for things to be all neatly wrapped up and finished, then I fear you will go away unsatisfied, since, at the Old Focus Home, life is mostly a matter of beginnings and continuing pursuits.

Thanks to Ms. Cromwell's shrewd coaching, our basketball team went on to the state finals, where we lost to a more experienced team from the mountains. But as a result of favorable publicity and community support, the School Board and the County Commissioners found money for another gym and an assistant coach at our school. Ms. Cromwell is planning to turn over her coaching responsibilities to the new person next year, not because it is too much for her, but because she is trying to get her women's track team in top shape for the Masters Tournament.

Ms. Smithers and two of her students won awards in the N.C. Artists Competition, and their works are now featured in the Museum of Art. Ms. Smithers' winning painting was an eight-by-ten-foot canvas of Shad and the Yellow House, as seen from the Peaceful River bridge. You feel as though you could walk right into the picture and find your way along the streets to the Old Focus Home. Some artists protested when so many awards went to one little bitty town, but Ms. Smithers' response to that was "You can't hide a light under a bushel." Whatever that means.

True to Ms. Nesselrode's prediction, JoAnne Preddy is not only playing for the premiere performance of *The New Symphonic Concertoratorio* but for all the other performances when the Symphony goes on tour. They have swapped places for the time being, with Ms. Nesselrode playing piano at the Methodist Church while JoAnne pursues a career. When Ms. Nesselrode is not teaching piano, she is learning Braille so she will be ready.

Dad, as manager of the Home, still talks to people about its practical aspects, but he refers all delegations and interested applicants to the ladies for a brief lecture on the importance of Friendship and Growing. He is not above mentioning the word "love" now and then, either. To give you some idea about how he is, I will just say that the girls on my team voted him the parent they most like to be around. He is the parent *I* most like to be around, too, but you could expect me to be prejudiced about that.

We held the dedication ceremony on the first day of May. It is a wonder the world did not tip over, so much of its population crowded into Shad for the event. Even though by now I am used to living in the midst of great activity, that occasion was almost too much for me, what with the ladies' friends, the governor, and other VIP's. It was like a society wedding or something. Late in the afternoon when everyone else was looking in another direction, I went down to the pier, got in our old leaky rowboat, and rowed out to the middle of the river. The further I moved from land, the more spacious the world became until finally it seemed there was enough room in it for me. I pulled in the oars and let the boat drift while I watched the sun go down.

It hung like a reluctant balloon just at the top of the line of trees on the opposite shore, then dropped suddenly out of sight, leaving the sky brilliant and the trees a mysterious greenish-black. The windows of houses winked pink and gold in the reflected light. Even weather-beaten wood took on a soft glow. The Yellow House, though still outstanding, was no longer the only bright spot in Shad. In those few moments the whole world seemed to flame like the hearts of the three ladies. Something bubbled up in me and I laughed, long and loud. The laughter echoed back and forth between trees and water and sky, and died away somewhere in the vicinity of sunset.

I fitted the oars back into the locks and rowed Home.

About the Author

SUZANNE NEWTON was born in Bunnlevel, Harnett County, North Carolina, and lived in several villages and towns before settling in Raleigh, in 1960.

Mrs. Newton graduated from Duke University in 1957 and taught English and French in Clarkton, North Carolina, for two years. She is married to Carl Newton and they have three daughters—Michele, Erin, and Heather—and a son, Craig. "All are avid readers," she says. "Music and books are staples of our family life."

Writing, for Mrs. Newton, is an adventure in self-discovery. For her, writing is not plotting and manipulating, but digging, discovery, and involvement.